Time Served in New York

CEE BOWERMAN

BOOK ELEVEN

This is a work of fiction. Names, characters, places, brands, media, and incidents are either the product of the author's imagination or are used fictitiously. Any resemblance to similarly named places or to persons living or deceased is unintentional.

Professionally edited by Chrissy Riesenberg

CEE BOWERMAN BOOK LIST

Texas Knights MC

Home Forever

Forever Family

Lucky Forever

Love Forever

Texas Kings MC

Kale

Sonny

Bird

Grunt

Lout

Smokey

Tucker

Kale & Terra (Novella)

John & Mattie

Bear

Daughtry

Hank

Fain

Grady

Conner Brothers Construction

Finn

Angus

Mace

Ronan

Royal - COMING APRIL 2021!

Rojo, TX

Rason & Eliza

Atlas & Addie

Time Served

Boss

Hook

Chef

Preacher

Captain

Bug

Santa

Kitty

Rodeo

Stamp
Time Served in New York

The Tempests

Wrath
Creed
Loki
Styx
Thorn
Freya
Sin-*Coming Dec 15th!*

The Donovans

Drink It Up
Pull It Up
Pretty It Up
Curl It Up

Please follow Cee on Facebook, Instagram, and Twitter.

Also, for information on new releases and to catch up with Cee, go to www.ceebowermanbooks.com

PANDORA

"You know planes have a weight limit, right?" Marler asked me from where he sat on the couch as he watched me sort and organize the clothes and shoes the girls wanted to take. "What you've got there on the table is enough for all of us to wear for six weeks without having to do any laundry."

I held up a cropped hoodie in one hand and a pair of ripped skinny jeans in the other before I tilted my head and said, "I don't know that these are really your aesthetic, but you can try them if you want."

Marler raised his eyebrows in question. "Do you think you'll have enough room for our clothes somewhere?" I looked at the coffee table and saw a stack of jeans beneath a stack of t-shirts with a pile of underwear on top of folded socks next to miniature versions of the same. "Jared and I could fit our shit into two plastic shopping bags and still have room for our toiletries."

I let out a sigh as my head fell back. I studied the ceiling for a second as my mind raced. "I haven't even gotten to that part yet."

"I've never been to a hotel that doesn't give you shampoo, soap, and lotion."

I lifted my head and stared at him as I thought of all the products me and the girls would need for our hair and faces along with the tools we used everyday. "That stuff isn't even . . . Just no, Marler."

"So we find a drugstore and buy some little bottles of your stuff when we get there. Easy peasy," he said with a shrug.

"That's not all we're taking for Jared . . . or you, for that matter."

"Yeah, it is. We're men, Pandora. Simple creatures who don't need much . . ."

"You need deodorant."

"Okay, I'll give you that one, but we could buy that at a pharmacy too."

"Do you know what the average temperature in New York City is during the month of December?" Marler shrugged. "It's in the 40s. That's why the girls packed their winter clothes instead of t-shirts."

"That was only half a shirt you held up a second ago," Marler pointed out. "Do their stomachs not get cold?"

"You were nice enough to pack Jared's things along with yours, and I appreciate that. However, a stack of t-shirts that Stamp has collected for him in his travels isn't really . . ."

"Well, that's what I'm wearing, and you think it's cute to make him all matchy-matchy and shit, so . . ."

"Marler, I swear I am going to . . ." Our argument was interrupted when the phone rang, and I snatched it up from the table as I glared at Marler while I tried to remember at least one thing I loved about him. When I glanced at the screen and saw it was Jenn calling, I greeted her with, "I hope to God you remember how to run the backhoe because we're gonna have to bury a body in about 10 minutes."

"Make that two," Jenn complained. "The man put his shit in the suitcase and then slid it across the bed and said, 'That's all the space you'll need, right?'"

"And then you killed him, huh?"

"I can't even fit the shoes I want to take in the space that's left!"

"Did he actually pack a coat or does he have a pile of jeans and t-shirts too?"

"Fuck. I never even considered the cold. That changes everything," Jenn groaned.

"Do I own a coat?" Marler asked as he stared at me with his head tilted.

"Does Boss own a coat?" Jenn asked at the same time.

"We don't leave until the day after tomorrow," Marler complained. "Can't we do this shit tomorrow night?"

"Let me call Paula and see what she's taking," Jenn said.

"I'll call Frankie and see how much space we actually have for luggage. Between us and the Ares women, we may need a cargo plane just for our bags."

"Text me after you talk to her," Jenn instructed before

she hung up.

I hit the button to speed dial Frankie and then put it on speaker before I set the phone down and listened to it ring. She finally answered.

"Hey, lady. I have a luggage question."

"It's funny that you called about that right now. I just told Christopher to call the guys to see if they wanted to go riding for a few hours. I need him to get out of my hair so I can pack."

I watched Marler perk up and laughed at the eager look on his face. I motioned toward the door, and he grinned as he jumped up and hurried around the table toward me. He gave me a kiss on the cheek accompanied by the usual ass grab and then he was out the door without so much as a backward glance.

"I should have thought of that two hours ago," I said as I flopped down on the chair. "Now I just need to figure out what to do with my kids." That very instant, a screaming fight started upstairs. "Fuck. I need a vacation."

"That's what this week is going to be - a vacation," Frankie assured me.

I laughed. "Obviously, you have no idea what it's like to try and entertain three teenagers and a toddler when you're crammed into a hotel room. And we're gonna be hauling them all over the place in a city with traffic unlike anything we've ever seen. If we go far, we'll need to take two cabs because . . ."

"Pandora . . ." Frankie tried to interrupt, but I was on

a roll and kept pouring out all my worries about my family being that far away from home.

"And how am I going to keep them entertained and show them the sights when I need to make sure I'm there for you? I looked online and found nanny services I can use while we're at the different things and all but . . ."

"Pandora . . ."

"They're strangers! Did you see that thing on the news a while back about the nanny that dropped the kids off . . ."

"Pandora! Shut up for a second, and let me talk," Frankie said firmly. I snapped my mouth shut at her sharpness, and she sighed. "Thank you. The plane is big enough to take whatever you can think of bringing. It's a commercial plane, not a private jet. When I told my brother how many people I needed to bring with me from Texas, he had to explore other options. As far as transportation inside the city, my brothers have that covered with vehicles and drivers. He's already purchased car seats for Jared and Boo, so they'll be perfectly safe. And . . . This is the best part . . . I just hired a housekeeper slash nanny who's gonna watch our two littles along with my youngest nephew while my older nieces and nephews show your girls around town."

"Alone? You want our kids to run around without adults all over Manhattan?" I squawked.

"Sweetheart, my nieces and nephews are never alone. They've each got a 24/7 guard. Believe me, they're not going to get up to anything we wouldn't condone."

"Oh." I let out a relieved breath. "And the nanny?"

"She's a student working on the thesis for her master's degree."

"We're gonna need heavy coats, aren't we?"

"Well, judging from the sudden left turn in conversation, I assume you're satisfied with the options offered for your children?"

I laughed before I said, "You sound so prim and proper sometimes. It cracks me up."

Frankie sighed. "Yes, you're going to need coats and gloves, at the very least. If you can cough up a scarf or two . . ."

"Fuck! I'm gonna send the girls a text and see who wants to go with me on a quick shopping spree."

"You're going to have to go to Dallas, but I've got the perfect store in mind. I'm already on vacation, so I'll come too," Frankie said with a tortured sigh. "If I hadn't already promised my brother I'd go through with this, I'd cancel and drag Christopher to Vegas for a quickie wedding like Bug and Maylee had."

"It's not too late. You can . . ."

"Absolutely not," Frankie interrupted with an odd laugh. "There's too much riding on this for me to cancel now."

"I don't want you to cancel just for the simple fact that you're going to force Blue to wear a dress and make Paula wear shoes for more than an hour at a time."

"It's not going to kill either one of them to deal, but

from the way they're bitching about it, I might murder them in the end anyway."

"And that is a show I'd pay to see."

KITTY

"Man, I'm so glad we got to take off for a bit. Jenn was making me crazy with the whole packing thing," Boss admitted as we sat down at a table inside The Hangout, the bar that the Ares Infidels MC owned in Tenillo. "And then there's her worry about the animals and all that. I get it, though. They're like our kids."

"Oh yeah," I agreed. "Thankfully, Pandora can leave Kama and Sutra in their habitat at the shop, and the girls that work for her know how to take care of them. But you guys have an entire menagerie to worry about."

"We're having them taken care of by a few of the guys that are staying behind. Fish and Chewie volunteered to take care of Pop and all the business matters while we're gone. Gizmo's still on parole, and there's not a chance in hell his PO would let him go fuck off in New York for a week."

"How much longer does he have?"

"About six months, I think."

"Hey, guys," Stamp said as he pulled out a chair and sat next to me. "Thanks for the invite. Birdie's making me nuts."

"Frankie's packing up the entire fucking house," Santa said as he sat down next to Boss. "It's enough to make me want to sweep her up and carry her to the fucking JP just to get this shit over with."

"I think we'd all greatly appreciate you doing that," I admitted. "You know, I've traveled all over the country for work and have *never* had to prep this much. Jared and I are easy, but the girls . . . Man, I'm glad we're taking a private plane because the amount of money I'd spend on excess baggage fees would break me if we flew commercial."

"What did I miss?" Preacher asked as he sat down.

"How's packing going for my sister?"

"Don't even get me started. She acts like we're leaving to sail around the world for a year. She's got a list of shit we need to take from Q-tips to hand sanitizer. I went to trim my fingernails this morning and searched the entire fucking house for the clippers only to find out she'd already packed them."

"Why?" Santa asked as he slowly shook his head.

"Said we might need them while we're there."

"Again, there are drugstores everywhere. Shit. You can get clippers at a convenience store," I said in exasperation. "Jeez. It's making me crazy enough that at this point, I'd welcome a trip to the nuthouse rather than Manhattan."

"Can I volunteer to escort you on that trip?" Executioner, one of the Ares Infidels, asked when he walked up to the table. "I had to escape. She acts like she's packing for us to go into an underground bunker for an unknown amount of time."

Preacher picked at his cuticle and muttered, "I should have grabbed the damn clippers out of my supply stash."

"Is this the escapee table?" Sin asked as he pulled a chair from a table nearby and slid it between Preacher and Boss. "If so, I'm down for whatever plan you've got."

"We could just take a road trip and pretend we got kidnapped," Executioner suggested. "Santa, you'll have to act as a witness since you're the only one who can't miss the New York trip."

"I'd rather be taken hostage at gunpoint than have to refold another goddamn t-shirt so everything fits in the suitcase."

"Suitcase? As in singular? I put my shit into one and was careful to leave enough room for Jenn, and she looked at me like I'd sprouted fucking horns. Who needs that much shit to go away for a week?"

I laughed at the exasperation in Boss's voice and said, "And they're out buying winter coats for us now."

"I never even thought about a coat," Sin said with a sigh. "Shit."

"You're gonna need a good one. We're playing golf," Stamp told him. "December in New York, and Birdie booked a tee time for us."

"I better pack some thermals, too, then," Executioner

said as he pulled his phone from his pocket. "Fuck. If I text her, she's gonna know I'm here talking to all of you and want me to pick up some shit before I come home."

"Just don't forget about it and slip some into the luggage when you get home later," I told him.

"You're right," Executioner agreed as he put his phone back down.

"Have you seen the schedule of events Birdie and Frankie have put together?" Stamp asked us.

"It's... a lot," Preacher said with a sigh. "Please, Santa, I'm begging you. Kidnap Frankie, take her to Vegas, find that Elvis impersonator Bug used, and marry her there. If you care about any of us at all, that's what you'll do."

"I'm with him, man," Sin said apologetically. "I never thought I'd encourage a kidnapping, but that's what I'm doing. Pick her up over your shoulder like a caveman, and just get in the truck and drive."

"I'll buy the fucking gas," Executioner offered.

"I'll give you the keys to Birdie's house on wheels," Stamp added. "Just shove her in there and go."

"Tie her up if you have to," Preacher suggested.

Boss nodded. "I'll loan you a pair of cuffs."

"I can call and make sure the fridge is stocked at our place there. Not a problem," I assured him.

Santa just shook his head as he stared forlornly at his beer. "This whole thing has snowballed into the wedding of the century, you guys. I can't stop it now."

"That clinches it," Preacher said. "I knew you hated us, you heartless, hairy bastard."

2

BLUE

"Why do I need a coat? Are we going hiking or something?"

"Blue, you're gonna be the death of me, I swear to God. How do you not own a winter coat?" Paula asked.

"When it gets cold here, we stay inside until it goes away. If I have to go out, it's a 10-second walk from the door to my truck. It takes longer than that for frostbite to set in."

"I've never owned a coat," Brea chimed in. "I want to find a really soft scarf with matching gloves."

Matalie perked up and said, "Neither have I. Oh! I want one of those long wool coats. Maybe a red one. With a houndstooth scarf and a furry black hat!"

I stared at Matalie like she'd lost her mind and asked, "Are you going to get a job standing outside the palace protecting the queen?"

"Why don't you get a red one too? You can get a job working at kids' birthday parties as Clifford with your Amazonian ass."

"I don't think I like you anymore. You were much nicer when we first met," I grumbled as I turned on my blinker to change lanes. "I'm not sure what happened."

"You! All of you happened! I was a really sweet girl when I moved to Tenillo. The other day, I almost ran over a woman with my grocery cart because she was walking too slow down the frozen aisle."

"I mean, I'm a nice person, but I plot people's death when they go slow in the left lane," Jenn confessed.

"That's perfectly normal," Brea said, and I heard the other women in the SUV agree. "Everyone does those things whether they want to admit it or not."

"Frankie, I just want you to know that you're testing the limits of our friendship in a big way," I told my friend as I glanced up at her reflection in the rearview mirror. "In two days, you'll have me in a metropolis with people . . . Ugh . . . Millions of people . . . all over the place. And not only are you going to make me go shopping in that big ass city and then wear a damn dress and heels for hours, but I also have to shop *today* and buy a fucking coat that I'm gonna wear for a week and then put in the back of my closet."

"Do you do anything without bitching about it for three weeks first? Anything? Ever?" Frankie stared at my reflection, daring me with an eyebrow raised. "I bet fifty dollars that you can't come up with a single thing."

"I don't bitch when Jude tells me to get naked because I like doing that," I said saucily. "Pay up, ho."

"Turn left at the light, Blue," Maylee said from the very back row of seats.

"I thought we were going to the mall."

"We are, just . . . not a regular kind of mall," Maylee

said cryptically.

I glared at her and then Frankie in the mirror. "What other kind of mall is there?"

"Let's just consider today's shopping adventure a test run for our trip," Frankie suggested.

"Why do we have to go to a fancy ass store for a fucking coat?" I asked.

"I've never actually seen a coat in a store around here," Brea mused. "Where could we even be going that would have one?"

"There's that ski shop at the mall. I bet they have them," Pandora suggested.

"Oh hell no," I whined after Maylee directed me to turn into the parking lot of a strip mall. "This is in the fancy neighborhood. Why do I suddenly feel like Julia Roberts?"

"Because you're a ho," Brea teased.

"She's a nice lady!" Paula shouted from where she was sitting beside Maylee. "I've got your back, Blue!"

"I don't think I can go on this trip," I complained. "I feel weak suddenly. I've got a sore throat, and my stomach is killing me."

"I saw you googling the symptoms of Ebola the other day, Blue. It's not going to work."

"Fucking doctors," I mumbled.

"I call shotgun for the ride home," Paula announced.

"Nope!" Jenn snapped. "You are not allowed anywhere near the stereo."

"What does she do with the stereo?" Maylee asked.

"She's a scanner. She never stops switching stations. It's like a tic," Jenn complained. "Makes me fucking nuts."

"Let her sit up front with Blue," I heard Brea suggest. "She'll slap the shit out of her hand if she even looks like she's thinking about touching the stereo."

"I make the loan payment, I choose the tunes," I explained. "Them's the rules."

"I'm not going to help you at all when we're inside then," Paula pouted as I parked the SUV in front of the store Frankie and Maylee had mentioned. "I'm going to tell the salesperson that you need special attention and can really only connect with a person if they're touching you."

"I'll touch *you,*" I threatened.

"Ladies, let's practice our manners while we're in here," Frankie said in a sugary sweet voice.

"Oh, this is gonna be awesome," Maylee said as she slid out.

"Assault charges that lead to more prison time are not on the shopping list," Matalie reminded us.

I sighed as I ran my hands over my face. I heard someone slap the hood and opened my eyes to find all seven women standing in front of the truck waiting on me.

"Find the coats and then retreat to your happy place,"

I whispered to myself as I got out. "You can do it. Channel your inner sweetheart."

I guess Brea heard me because she laughed for a second before she said, "I don't think they sell new personalities here."

MAYLEE

I smiled at the attendant who'd delivered my champagne and held the glass aloft, waiting for Frankie and Paula to join me in a toast. "Welcome to the show, ladies. Let the games begin."

Paula laughed before she took a sip. "I can't wait to get these girls to the city. It's gonna be awesome."

"I looked over the itinerary Bernadette sent and saw that there should be some downtime for sightseeing."

"There will be plenty of time," Frankie assured me before she took another sip. She leaned forward and took a fresh strawberry from the tray the saleswoman had set on the ottoman in front of the couch where we were sitting and studied it for a second before she took a bite. After another sip of champagne, she said, "I have a list of places I think we should go. Bernadette's been helping me."

"I have a few suggestions," I told the women before I giggled at the look of horror on Blue's face. The saleswoman was showing her a selection of coats she'd brought out in Blue's size, and I could tell just at a glance that none of them would do. "How long are we going to pretend that this is the only place with a selection of winter wear?"

Frankie laughed wickedly and then grinned as Matalie spun around wearing a floor-length red cape that was more suited for an evening gala than a day of sightseeing in brisk weather. "I say we have about half an hour before Blue starts twitching, and then we can go over to that ski shop Pandora mentioned."

I selected a chocolate truffle from the selection on the tray and took a bite. "I have the perfect long red overcoat for Matalie to borrow. I believe I even have a houndstooth scarf."

"I store all of my winter clothes at Ziggy's, so he had someone deliver them to the hotel this afternoon. I've got at least a dozen coats for them to choose from, and there are gloves and scarves to match all of them."

"Oh shit. We're horrible people," Paula mused when we heard Brea ask the saleswoman for the price of the coat she was wearing. Brea's mouth dropped open in shock, and she stood there stunned for a second before she sucked in a deep breath and started coughing. "That's fucking hilarious."

Brea carefully took off the coat and handed it to the saleswoman before she said something to Matalie who was still twirling around in her cape. Matalie's eyes got as wide as saucers, and she stopped so suddenly that the cape swirled around her legs, tripping her as she walked toward Blue who was trying on a dark gray overcoat.

"This costs *how much?*" Blue shouted as she let the coat

slide off her shoulders.

"Shit. I was hoping to be able to finish my champagne before she lost it," Frankie said sullenly. She got up and walked toward the counter as she called out, "Let me pick up the gifts I ordered for my niece and then we can go."

Blue's face was stormy as she stomped in our direction. "What sort of place is this anyway?"

"It's a boutique that has coats," I said calmly. "That's what you all need."

"That coat I had on is more than my mortgage payment," Blue hissed. "And it's ugly as fuck!"

"You did look a little like Inspector Gadget," Paula said with a grin. "Want some champagne?"

"Where the fuck did you get champagne?" Brea asked as she reached for Paula's glass.

"They serve it to their clientele," I explained. "It's always . . ."

"Oh my hell, that's delicious," Brea said before she took another sip.

"I am *not* spending two grand on a fucking cape," Matalie said as she snatched the champagne out of Brea's hand. "I'll freeze to death first."

"You looked like Little Red Riding Hood," Pandora told her. "I liked it."

"I did, too, until I heard how much the damn thing cost."

Frankie returned with a large bag, and I could see gift-wrapped boxes inside. "Okay, we can go now. I've gotten what I came for."

"Really?" Blue barked.

"I ordered some things for my niece," Frankie explained with a shrug. "I've got a ton of coats for all of you to choose from. There's no sense in buying new ones."

"You are such a bitch," Blue hissed.

"Matalie, I have a red coat that will look stunning on you. I don't think you looked like Red Riding Hood at all."

"And you were in on it!" Blue said angrily.

Matalie glared at me and then her eyes brightened when she asked, "Do you have a scarf and hat too?"

"Scarf, yes. Furry hat? Definitely not."

"Two out of three ain't bad," Matalie said as she followed Frankie and Blue toward the door. "Now I just have to find coats for Auggie and Rodeo."

"What about the girls?" Brea asked.

"They're going to stay home with their other grandparents. August and Rodeo are considering this trip their honeymoon."

"That's cool," Pandora said. "We should all pitch in and send them on a night out with dinner at a really nice restaurant."

"I'll get my son to arrange something," Paula assured

her.

"Make sure you warn Rodeo about the bathroom situation," Frankie reminded Paula. "As a matter of fact, while we're on the plane we should have a . . . talk . . . a discussion about . . . um . . ."

"Wow, she's just sputtering right through that, isn't she?" Blue teased.

Brea hummed before she asked, "Do you think she's trying to find a nice way to say they need to educate the rednecks?"

"I think she's trying to find a way to subtly remind people they can't shank anyone," Blue suggested.

Frankie looked at me and shook her head in exasperation, "It's going to be like someone left the gates of Jurassic Park open and let the beasts invade Manhattan."

"That's been done already, hasn't it?" Blue asked.

"I don't think so," Matalie answered. "They're always at some exotic location. Oh wait! Maybe one of them was in Central Park!"

"Right," Paula said sarcastically. "Because that's an exotic location."

"Woman, hush. Everything I know about Central Park I learned from *Stuart Little* and *Spider-Man,*" Blue snapped.

"An American Tale," Jenn said with a sappy look. *"Somewhere out there . . ."*

When the other women, Paula and Frankie included, started singing the theme song to the movie, I glanced over at the saleswomen who were huddled near the counter and laughed at their mortified expressions.

As I followed the singing women out of the boutique, I couldn't help but think that this next week was going to be one hell of an adventure.

SANTA

"Are you in charge of the baggage?" I asked a man who was standing on the tarmac watching some other men sort through the luggage that everyone had set in the area cordoned off near the rear of the plane.

He looked like he didn't belong there and seemed to be scrutinizing the crews' every move.

"I'm a private employee. I don't work for the airline," the man said flatly. "You're Mr. Miller?"

"That's me," I said as I stuck my hand out to shake his. "You can call me Santa."

"You're joking, right?"

"No, that's actually what I go by," I assured him.

The man glanced over at the large plastic bin I'd helped Stamp and a few of the other guys secure a few days ago before he said, "I find your name ironic considering you're delivering a very nice gift to my employers just a few weeks before Christmas."

I laughed when I realized how funny that sounded and shrugged, "At least there aren't any reindeer involved, right?"

"I appreciate that."

"Is there anything you need us to do?"

"Not a thing. I've got it from here."

"Thank you. I'm sure I'll see you again when we get to New York."

"No, you won't," the man said as he shook my hand again and glanced back at the luggage. He smiled, but it didn't reach his eyes as he warned, "You didn't even see me here."

BREA

"How many times have you flown, Marques? It's going to be okay, I promise."

"I've flown at least a hundred times, but it doesn't get any easier," he mumbled before he leaned forward and rested his head on the seat in front of us. "The trainers always gave me some kind of pill when we met at the airport."

"Just take some deep breaths in through your nose," I said as I rested my hand on his back and tried to soothe him.

"You're gonna be fine," I heard Blue say from somewhere behind us. "People fly all the time, Jude."

"There's a reason man doesn't have wings, Blue,"

Preacher growled in return. "If I was fucking meant to fly, we'd be sweeping feathers off the floor every day."

"He's so dramatic," I heard Sis whisper from her seat behind me.

I kept rubbing Marques's back but twisted around to look at my daughter. "Which one?"

Sis sighed and lifted her hand up to point at Soda who was unconscious in the seat next to hers. He let out a soft snore right before she explained, "He's never flown before. He's also never taken melatonin. As you can see, he's doing great at both."

"If we're going to join the Mile High Club, I want to do it now," I heard my friend Sara whisper as she walked past me.

"Let's get settled in first . . ."

Sara looked back at Trident and hissed, "You know we're not the only ones thinking it, and I'm not sure I'll want to after someone else."

"Good point, my heart. Drop your bags and meet me in the lavatory at the rear of the plane. We'll hide out until takeoff."

I twisted back around and saw the horrified look on Sis's face and knew she'd overheard the same conversation. I had to put my hand over my mouth to stifle the laughter and felt my eyes filling with tears.

"Oh Brea," Bernadette said as she stopped at the end of our aisle and took in my damp eyes. "Are you okay? Do you want me to sit with you? I'll hold your hand or . . . What can I do?"

"Birdie, she's fine," Stamp insisted as he nudged her from behind. "Let's go sit down."

"But she's . . ." Bernadette looked shocked when Sis started laughing behind me. I couldn't hold it in any more and leaned forward to rest my forehead on the seat in front of me as I let go of the laughter I'd been trying to hold in.

"I'm sorry . . . oh shit!" I heard Sis snort and then laugh even harder.

"Excuse me, guys," Sin, the president of the Ares men, said as he tried to squeeze past Bernadette and Stamp. "Front bathroom's taken, and I need to . . ."

Sis and I stood up at the same time, and I put my hand on Sin's arm. "No! You can't go back there! It's . . ."

"Occupied!" Sis finished for me. "There's a line!"

"Yeah! Wait for the front one!"

Sin tilted his head and studied us before his eyes narrowed. He looked toward the back of the plane and got a horrified look on his face. When I glanced over my shoulder, I saw Sara smiling as she walked into the lavatory, and then Trident's face appeared right before the door shut.

Sin made a retching sound and put his hand over his mouth. I yanked the airsick bag out of the pocket on the seatback in front of me and slapped it against his chest with one hand while I spun him around with the other. "Just don't think about it, Sin."

Sin clutched the bag in one hand and kept the other over his mouth as he walked back toward the front of the plane where he was sitting with some of the other Ares men and women.

Stamp had his lips clamped together, trying not to laugh, but he lost it when Bernadette whispered, "Oh God! Isn't that his mom?"

After Stamp and Bernadette walked past us to find a seat, I sat back down and focused on Marques. "Honey, are you gonna be sick? I don't know what to do for you."

"I just need to chill here for a bit. I'll be okay once we get . . . Ugh. . . I think I'm gonna stay home," Chef said suddenly as he sat straight up in his seat. He nodded and started to stand, but I stopped him with my hand on his arm. "Pickle, you go on without me. I'll make it on my own."

"You sound like we're leaving you in enemy territory or something," Sis grumbled.

"Here," Paula said as she appeared and thrust her hand out toward Marques. "Eat this." Chef looked at her hand and then up at her face in question. "I didn't give Sis melatonin for Soda. In about 15 minutes, Preacher's gonna be seeing life-sized gummy bears and giggling like a schoolgirl. If you eat this, you can join him on that trip."

Marques took it from her and popped it into his mouth. He swallowed it without even chewing and said, "I'm a big man. Give me another."

Paula raised her eyebrows and looked over at Soda, who was drooling with his head resting against the window. "Yeah, I don't think that's a good idea."

"He ate all three of them," Sis explained with an exaggerated wince. "He said he wanted to make sure he didn't make an ass out of himself sprinting toward the emergency exit before we take off."

"Give me another one," Marques ordered with his hand out.

"If you end up like him, how are we gonna get the two of you off the fucking plane?" Paula asked.

"She has a point. You and Hook are the biggest . . . "

"Hook's sitting behind Blue and Preacher waiting for the gummy bear show to start," Paula explained. "He took one about five minutes ago."

"That means *you* are the only one big enough to carry Soda off this plane," I explained. "The other guys might be able to get Hook, but Soda's a big boy."

"I think you should donate your second gummy to Sin," Sis suggested. "He probably needs it more than you do."

"Why?"

I grinned at Paula before I motioned toward the back of the plane. "He saw Sara going into the bathroom with Trident."

Paula's laugh was evil as she took her container of gummies and walked toward the front of the plane where Sin and Lyric were sitting.

"Ladies and gentlemen, the last passengers have boarded, and the flight crew is prepared for take off," the flight attendant announced.

"Shit!" Marques agonized before he buckled the seat belt across his lap. He tightened it so much that I was worried about his circulation, but I didn't say anything because he leaned his head back and in a frantic whisper started chanting, "I'm not gonna die today."

I saw Paula hurrying down the aisle toward me and put my hand up to stop her. "Give me another one."

Without a word, Paula popped the container open and handed me a square gummy before she rushed toward the back of the plane where Hook was waiting for her.

"Marques, chew this time. It might make it digest faster."

Sis chimed in from behind me, "Maybe he should hold it under his tongue so it dissolves or something."

Marques kept his eyes closed and just let his mouth drop open and stuck his tongue out.

"It's gonna be okay, big guy," Sis said as she reached between the seats and put her hand on his shoulder. "We'll take care of you."

I buckled my seat belt as the attendant walked toward me and then I took Marques's hand. He clutched mine like a lifeline, so I leaned against his shoulder and slowly rubbed his chest as the plane started moving to get into position for takeoff.

"Love you, Pickle."

"I love you, too, Marques. It's going to be over before

you know it," I reassured him.

That prompted more than one of our friends to shout, "That's what she said!"

BERNADETTE

"How are you doing, Birdie?" Valentine asked once the plane took off and everyone started mingling and talking again.

"I'm fine. I don't mind flying."

"That's not what I'm talking about," Valentine said as he reached for my hand. "We're going home and . . ."

"My home is in Texas with you."

"You know what I mean," Valentine pressed. "You haven't gone back without watching over your shoulder for years. How are you feeling about that?"

"I'm excited. I'll get to see Carol and check on my house. And I can't wait to go to Westchester Square and get donuts from this . . ."

"Westchester? You're from the Bronx?"

"You're just now figuring that out?"

Valentine laughed softly and shook his head. "I know you said you were thinking about selling your house since

Carol's moving and won't be able to keep an eye on it, but if it's in the Bronx, my boys can make sure everything's okay for you."

"Oh, I'd hate for them to go out of their way."

"They live in Manhattan now, but their, um . . . work is in the Bronx."

"Depending on where they work . . ."

"The Bronx *is* their work," he explained. "Just like Frankie's family *works* Queens, and Paula's son *works* Brooklyn."

"I'm so disconnected from home that I never really considered their *work.* I mean, I grew up there, so I know what goes on but . . ." Valentine's soft laugh interrupted me. "Okay, so I don't *know* really, but you get what I mean." We were quiet for a bit, listening to our friends talking, before I finally asked what had been on my mind since we arrived at the airport. "Is he . . . here?"

"Who?"

I tilted my head and frowned. "Is *he* on the plane? You know . . . With the luggage."

Valentine burst out laughing and then stifled it and tried to look somber before he answered, "Yes, he is."

"How did you do that?" I asked in total awe. "I can't even get through TSA without myself and my bag being molested, but you got *him* on the plane without them so much as blinking an eye?"

"We're on a private charter, Birdie. We didn't go

through TSA, remember?"

"Right . . . but . . ."

"We drove the luggage directly onto the tarmac and loaded it into the plane. I'm sure Frankie's brother has men working the hold that he trusts."

"He owns this plane?"

"No. From what Frankie said, he rented it for our trip. But that doesn't mean he's not in control of who's handling our luggage."

"Oh."

"It's going to be okay, Birdie. I promise."

"I'll be glad to know he's nowhere near our home," I admitted. "I was walking over to Jenn's the other day and saw that the, um, landscape looked different, so I knew that . . ."

Valentine smiled as he interrupted. "You don't have to say anything. Just know that it's all taken care of, and in about four hours, we'll have washed our hands of the whole situation. You can rest easy, and at some point, so can Carol."

"I love you, Valentine. Thank you for taking care of me."

"Thank you for letting me, Birdie. I love you too."

4

BLUE

"Did you see the bathtub?" I heard Matalie ask August as I sat across the table from them.

I'd already filled my plate at the breakfast buffet along the far wall and leaned back when a woman in a hotel uniform filled the empty mug in front of me from the steaming carafe she held. When I glanced up and said, "Thank you, ma'am," she looked taken aback before she smiled.

"I got into it fully dressed and told Tyler we're moving in for good," August answered, still talking about the tub in her room. She continued with a grin, "He said that even if he went back to stripping full-time, we wouldn't be able to afford a week here."

"The nanny that Frankie arranged for us is taking care of the kids in one of the penthouse suites," Lyric explained. "She took us up and . . . it was so . . . I mean, it's just . . ."

"The nanny stole your ability to speak in exchange for getting the prince to fall in love with you?" I blurted when Lyric stammered as she tried to come up with an accurate description. "Holy shit. Where the fuck did that come from?"

Everyone laughed before Brea said, "He's rubbing off on her."

"He's rubbing something," Paula teased.

"Next thing you know, they're going to start prepping for the apocalypse," Jenn said with a bark of laughter. When she saw the look on my face, she gasped, "No! Really?"

"He bought these buckets full of MREs . . ."

"The envelopes of dehydrated food?" Sis asked. "He invited me and Soda over for dinner and then went on and on about how easy they are to prepare and how they would last forever. When I sat down at the table, he had a carafe of hot water and a variety for us to try."

"Worse than prison food?" Matalie asked with a grimace.

"A few of them weren't that bad," I admitted before Sis looked at me like I was insane. "I'm serious!"

"She's further down the rabbit hole than we thought. We may need to stage an intervention," Brea said seriously. "There was a kitchen fire while I was in prison, and they made us eat those until the remodel was finished. Let me just say that the Geneva Convention should add MREs to the list of unspeakable crimes."

"We've got to get a move on," Lyric said from the doorway. "We're going sightseeing with the guys while y'all go over the last of the wedding details."

"Are you sure Desi will be okay with the other kids?" Sara asked Frankie as she made her way to the door.

"My nieces and nephews will take good care of her," Frankie said assuringly. "And Pandora's girls are with them, too, so it's not like she's alone."

"Where are they going?"

"They're taking them on a movie tour," Frankie replied. "My nephews helped plan it. They're going to visit all the iconic places that have been in the Marvel movies and a bunch of others too."

"Is it too late for me to go with them?" I asked. "What? I love *Iron Man*."

"You love his chauffeur," Brea corrected.

"He's an adorable teddy bear," I snapped.

"We've got to go too," August said as she stood up. "We're supposed to meet downstairs in 10 minutes, right?"

"Yes. The concierge is expecting you. He'll introduce you to your drivers for the day."

Once we said goodbye to the Ares women and settled in for our planning session, Frankie surprised us by saying, "I thought we could go exploring after we finish breakfast."

"Downstairs? The list of boutiques just here in the hotel is astounding," Matalie said.

"I actually thought you guys might like to walk through the park on our way to Fifth Avenue for some shopping before the appointment for our dress fittings."

"We're going to Fifth Avenue?" Maylee asked in a shocked whisper before she admitted, "I don't hate you nearly as much as I did when you said this week would be full of wedding activities."

"Right off the bat, we're going shopping?" I asked.

"Do you *want* to get married with a broken nose?"

"Hear me out," Frankie said, putting her hands up as if to ward off danger. "We're going to take our time and walk through the park, then walk down Fifth Avenue before we cross over to the bridal shop on Lexington."

"And that's good, why?"

"My hope, unfortunately for some poor innocent person out there, is that we will come upon a mugging or maybe even an old-fashioned purse snatching. You ladies can chase the asshole down, beat him half to death, and then be mellow for at least a few hours."

Jenn looked confused when she asked, "You hope we come across someone being mugged so Blue can beat the shit out of them and that will make her behave while we're in the store?"

"Hmm. That might actually help me too," Brea admitted. "I'm not really a shopper either."

"Neither is Paula," Frankie agreed. "My thinking is that the three of you can work out your aggression while we hold your coffee and then we can go to the store and have a few cocktails while we get fitted."

"What happens if we don't find a mugger?" I asked.

"I've planned for that," Bernadette chimed in. "If you can behave while we're in the store, you'll get treats and we'll take you somewhere special when we're finished."

I glared at Bernadette for a second before she turned and looked at Frankie for help. Frankie chimed in, "Just a few hours of shopping and then we'll go ride the subway until you feel better."

"The subway's gonna make her feel better?" Paula asked, her head tilted in confusion.

"Where else can we take her where no one will look twice when she loses her shit and starts screaming at someone because they looked in her direction a smidge too long?"

"The subway is where all the really crazy stuff happens!" Jenn said excitedly. "This is going to be so much fun!"

"You don't have any weapons on you, do you?" Bernadette asked.

Rather than look at me, Frankie gave Paula a pointed look and asked, "Do *you?*"

"What? I didn't say shit."

"Paula. Weapons?"

"You're gonna put us on a train in the middle of New York, and you think I shouldn't go armed? Are you already drunk?"

"Especially if we're carrying bags from all these fancy stores," I added. "Are you trying to get *us* mugged?"

"We'll have whatever we buy delivered to the hotel," Bernadette explained.

"I saw a pair of red-soled slingbacks online that I have to have," Maylee announced. "I bet they have them at Berg's."

"The ones you sent me that pic of that cost almost a grand?" Matalie gasped. "You were fucking serious?"

"They'd be the perfect shoes to wear to the wedding," Maylee argued. "I showed Frankie, and she agreed."

"Out of all of us, you're the craziest," Matalie said as she shook her head. "Total fucking nutjob."

"We *will* have to do our shoe shopping before the dress fittings just to make sure everything is measured correctly," Frankie said with an excited grin.

"We're going to try on shoes?" Matalie asked, her entire demeanor changing in an instant. "Really?"

"Prozac, don't fail me now! If someone punches you in the face, do they still have to go to your wedding? I'm asking for a friend," I lied.

"Me! She's asking for me," Brea chimed in.

"If we have to do this, then why aren't you punishing Sis and August? They're part of the coven too! It's not fair," Paula wailed.

"Since they're not in the wedding, I arranged for both couples to have a few romantic days together," Bernadette explained.

"I need romance!" Paula shouted. "Hook and I are on the verge of separation. We should spend some quality time alone together."

"You lying skank!" Jenn argued. "I caught the two of you banging in the elevator not two hours ago!"

"We were . . . working on our deep-seated issues."

"Oh, something was deep. I'm just saying," Jenn mumbled.

"The concierge told me there were complaints about you and Boss getting busy on your balcony," Frankie said primly. "Apparently, the people in the residential building next door got quite a show last night and *then again* this morning."

"We were exploring our love of nature," Jenn shot back.

Matalie laughed and confessed, "We did that too."

Frankie leaned forward and rested her elbows on the table before she put her face in her hands. "It's like someone made a movie about the Clampetts taking over New York, and I'm right in the fucking middle of it."

"Did you just call us hillbillies?" Jenn asked.

"They were in Beverly Hills, Frankie. Wrong television show."

Frankie lifted her head and stared at me for a second before she said, "If you don't stop fucking around and get on board with this bullshit, I'm going to drown every single one of you in the Hudson River and tell your men you were kidnapped by . . . Fuck! I don't know who, but I'll come up with something!"

"Come on!" Bernadette said as she stood up. She clapped her hands together and then started walking toward the double doors. "It's starting to look like Frankie could use a mugger too."

"I'm so excited!" Maylee exclaimed.

"About beating the shit out of someone in the park? Really?"

"The shoe shopping, Blue. Seriously."

"Matalie is right. You are the craziest one out of all of us."

PAULA

"If shopping was always like this, I don't think I'd mind it so much," Brea admitted from where she was sprawled on the floor next to Blue. She lifted her head up just enough to take another sip of champagne and then put the drink down gently and let her head thump back onto the carpet. "I could get used to this. This town's not half bad."

"I could do without trekking through the forest to get where I want to go, but that park wasn't horrible. No muggers, though. It's probably too cold out." I shook my head when Blue hiccupped, burped, then hiccupped again. "I'm a fan of this whole drinking while we shop thing."

"You two have been laying on the floor for damn near an hour. How is that shopping?" Maylee said as she slipped on yet another pair of heels.

"You've got a foot fetish," Pandora slurred. "I've

never seen someone get so turned on by shoes."

"Retifism is different from podophilia," Maylee said as she stood and walked toward the mirror where she turned to the side and posed, staring at the shoes in her reflection.

"I don't know what either of those are, but sure," Blue agreed.

"Those are fetishes," Maylee explained. "Retifism is what you would call a shoe fetish and podophilia is a foot fetish. They can go hand in hand or be totally separate."

"How do you know shit like that?" Blue asked as she rolled to her side and propped her head up on her hand. She looked at Brea who was lying on her back beside her and asked, "Why would someone know that?"

"Knowing those kinds of things was integral to my job," Maylee explained.

"I bet you saw some wild shit," Matalie said as she stood up with *another* pair of shoes on and walked over to model them in the mirror beside Maylee. "What's the weirdest kink you ever encountered?"

Maylee grimaced. "You'll have to be more specific. Most of them are what I would consider weird, but to each his own, right?"

"What's the funniest thing a john ever asked you to do?" I asked.

Maylee thought about it for a second and then laughed. "I had this one guy who got off when I washed his hair."

"Huh?"

"He had this sink set up in the bathroom of his penthouse that had a sprayer just like a salon. He'd sit in that chair fully-clothed, and I'd wash his hair wearing just my bra and panties."

"And he paid you for that?"

"Very well," Maylee replied. "He had another little . . . preference . . . that I charged an outrageous amount for. It's something called axillism."

"What's that?"

Maylee grinned wickedly, and I knew that whatever she said was going to make the women on the floor go nuts. "I wasn't allowed to shower for a solid 24 hours before the appointment."

"And? I mean, that's kinda gross but . . ."

"I couldn't wear deodorant," Maylee interrupted. It took less than two seconds for her words to sink in and everyone in the room reacted. Maylee wasn't finished, though, and talked over their grumblings and groans of disgust. "*And,* when I was finished with his hair, he had sex with my armpit."

The room exploded, and Maylee had to lean over and brace her hand on the chair to hold herself up through her laughter.

"How much did he pay for *that?*" Brea asked.

"Ten thousand a session," Maylee chortled.

"10k?" Blue said as she sat straight up and stared at Maylee in shock. "No!" When Maylee just nodded, Blue said, "I can't go without deodorant, but I'd let someone fuck my armpit for ten grand too. For that much money, I think I could even get Jude to go for it."

"Shit. For that much money, you might be able to get Preacher to film it," I added.

"How does . . . I mean . . . Where does that come from?" Jenn asked from the chair next to the one where Maylee was now sitting and dabbing the corners of her eyes. "Did he wake up one day and think, 'Sweaty armpits are *hot!*' and then just roll with it?"

"Ms. Romano, would you like me to put that pair aside for you?" the elegantly dressed saleswoman said without even breaking stride.

"Anna! I bet you have some stories!" Matalie said as she stared at the saleswoman that she, Pandora, and Blue had made friends with almost as soon as we walked into the store. "Tell us something good."

"Oh, I'm not sure I have anything that can compare to . . ." Anna paused and put her hand up to her mouth as she swallowed a few times and then gagged. "*. . . that.*"

"Have you seen some shoe fetish freaks? You have, huh?" I asked.

"I do have a client that thoroughly enjoys it when me and some of the other saleswomen model the latest shoes," Anna admitted. "I'm sure it's nothing sexual, though."

"Oh, you know it is," Blue teased. "Come on, Anna!

Spill the tea!"

"Some of the women appreciate the tips they receive if they let him take pictures of their feet in the shoes they model."

"I knew it!" Blue cheered. "How much does he tip?"

Anna shook her head and glanced over her shoulder to make sure no one else could hear when she said, "He gives us each a thousand dollars if we let him take a couple of shots, and of course, we get the commission when he buys the shoes we've modeled."

"He shops here, so he must be loaded," Brea whispered. "I wonder who it is!"

"He only comes to visit a few times a year unless he's on location for an extended amount of time," Anna hinted. "That's all I'm going to tell you."

"He's an actor," Pandora concluded. Anna didn't answer. She just smiled as she took the shoes from Frankie and walked away. "Now I have to figure out who she's talking about."

"Okay, that's enough about shoes and weirdos," Bernadette said as she stood up from her chair. "Let's go try on our dresses!"

"I'm drunk. You're gonna have to drag me," Blue said as she flopped back to the floor.

"I'll do it," Jenn said as she walked over to Blue's feet. "Come on, Paula. We're pretty good at this."

"You can do it, put your back into it!" I sang as I jumped

up and stood next to Jenn. Blue lifted her legs so we could each grab an ankle and then sang the rest of the lyrics in an off-key voice with us along with Pandora, Matalie, and Brea, *"You can do it, put your ass into it!"*

"Hillbillies!" Frankie hissed before she picked up the champagne and took a long swig straight from the bottle. She wiped her mouth with the back of her hand and then let out a delicate burp before she scowled at the women in the middle of the room. "I'm surrounded by hillbillies!"

JENN

"Do you think the guys are having as much fun as us?" Paula asked as she sat down next to me. We were wearing robes that the saleswoman had given us when she asked us to get undressed so she could take our measurements. We were even wearing matching slippers as we refreshed our flutes of champagne. "I can't imagine that it's taken them this long to get measured for their tuxes."

"How do you think they are gonna handle it when some man gets all up in their junk to measure their inseams?" I asked.

"I'd guess that at least one of them has already committed assault and battery," Matalie said as she sat in the chair beside mine. "I thought about warning Gus but then decided it would make a funnier story if I didn't."

"I just got a text from Jude," Blue said from where she was sprawled on the floor with Brea and Paula. "He said they're almost finished at the tuxedo shop and then they're coming over here."

"Frankie's dress is put away, right?" Bernadette asked as she hopped up from her chair. "I'll make sure."

"Where's Maylee?" Blue asked.

"She's in there trying . . ." My voice trailed off when Maylee appeared in the arched doorway. "Oh, Maylee, you look beautiful!"

"They had to pull out all the stops on the bodice," Maylee explained as she ran her hands down the front of the dress. "My shoes match *perfectly!*"

We watched as Maylee lifted the hem of her dress and stuck her foot out. "You're going to leave those with the dress for now, aren't you?" Frankie asked as she walked in, still in her robe too.

"I'll take them to the hotel with me . . ."

"She's gonna show Bug and then they're gonna get busy while she wears her shoes," Paula said knowingly. "Probably gonna use some of that pretty underwear we found earlier too."

Maylee scoffed as she rolled her eyes. "Sweetheart, I'm always wearing exquisite lingerie."

"The rest of the guys are lucky we put on pants everyday, and then there's Bug who knows *all* of Victoria's secrets," I teased.

"I wear pants all the time!" Paula argued.

"Cookie Monster pajamas are not pants," Blue argued.

"Says the woman who has sweatpants featuring the Rugrats characters," Paula argued. "At least I wear a bra . . . sometimes."

Frankie let the women argue about their clothing choices and plopped down beside me. "They're like drunk children."

"I know, right?" I said as I tried to focus on her face. "Damn kids."

"You're as drunk as I am, and you know it."

"Maybe."

Frankie and I watched as Matalie got on the floor with the other women as Maylee walked back into the dressing area. Bernadette appeared and walked toward us with a smile. "Both dresses will be put away so Santa won't see them."

"I should let him see it so my brother will have to buy me another one," Frankie said bitterly.

"You've already got two!" I argued. "Who has two dresses?"

"One is for the ceremony, and the other is for the reception. They're both beyond compare, but my wedding dress is more ornate and . . . bigger. You saw it. It's got its own zip code, and there's enough material there to make curtains for every window in my house. It's ridiculous and so not me at all."

"Can I ask a personal question?" Frankie looked at me and shrugged. "It's obvious that you're not into this huge wedding thing. Why are you going through with it and costing your brother . . ."

"And Paula's brothers, her son, Stamp's kids . . ." Frankie interrupted.

I tilted my head in confusion. "Why are they paying for your wedding?"

"My brothers want to see me get married, of course, but the wedding represents something even bigger than just *my* future," Frankie explained. "It's the future of the four families together. My wedding is the perfect venue for them to prove they're happily working together instead of going for each other's throats."

"Is that normal?"

"For them to be in the same room?" Paula had moved closer to us while the other women laughed on the floor, and she explained, "Stamp killed my uncle after he gunned down Stamp's dad and sister."

"*That's* normal, or at least it has been in the past. The four families are working together now, and my wedding is the perfect way to showcase that. All of the different factions will be in attendance along with the other major families from up and down the coast who are becoming allies with the new Italian group."

"How many undercover feds do you think will find their way in?" Paula asked.

"My guess is at least 20," Bernadette chimed in.

"How do the older generations feel about the new direction your brothers and the kids are taking things?" I asked.

Paula shrugged. "You know what Zach and my brothers did to secure his spot. Stamp's boys and Frankie's brothers helped with that too."

"The ones that are still around didn't have a choice in the matter," Frankie explained. "In some instances, their names are the only thing keeping them alive."

"Their names?"

Bernadette nodded. "Most everyone knows all of the family members by sight. Well, the men at least. Other times, it's all in the name."

"People are afraid of others because of their name?" I asked. "I've read about shit like that, but I seriously thought it was strictly fiction."

A different saleswoman walked into the room with another bucket of champagne and a tray of fruits and cheeses. I recognized her as the snotty woman who had said something snarky to Matalie earlier. I knew Paula was up to something when she winked at me and said, "It's been a while since I've done it but watch this."

"What . . ."

"Can I get you anything else, ladies?" the saleswoman asked as she glanced at our friends who were giggling on the floor.

"I had the woman assisting us hold a negligee for me

earlier, but I'm not sure I told her my room number at the Castello," Paula said with a smile that was obviously fake. "I've had so much champagne that I'm not sure I remember the room number."

"That's not a problem," the saleswoman said with a smile that was also clearly disingenuine. "What name is the room registered under? We can have it delivered that way."

"Paola Moretti," Paula said as she stared directly into the woman's eyes. She tilted her head and laughed softly before she let out a dramatic sigh. "If all else fails, have it delivered to my son's office in the building. His name is Zachary Campana."

The woman gulped and blinked a few times as she took a step back. She smiled, and this time it wasn't condescending at all. There was nothing but respect and awe in her voice when she said, "Of course, Ms. Moretti. We'll make sure it's delivered directly to you."

"Oh, and will you please make sure the night serum I picked out is delivered to my room?" Bernadette asked. The saleswoman's eyes snapped over to Bernadette, and I could tell she was wracking her brain trying to figure out if she should know her too. "It's under Valentine Russo, I'm sure."

The woman's eyes were practically bulging now, and I almost felt sorry for her. Almost but not quite. She'd been a snotty bitch to all of us up until about two minutes ago.

"Actually, all of the rooms are listed under my family's name," Frankie said. "If you'll speak to the concierge, he'll assist you in having their packages delivered to the floor reserved for Mr. Romano's guests. We'll get them sorted out once they arrive."

"Yes, Ms. Romano," the woman said with a nod. She looked as if she was considering a curtsy as she asked Frankie, "Can I do anything else for you?"

"That is all," Paula said with a dismissive wave. Once the woman scurried out of the room, Paula closed her hand and breathed on her nails before she buffed them against her chest. "I think I've still got it."

"I'm pretty sure she peed a little," Matalie said before she collapsed back to the floor, giggling. "I really needed friends like you in prison."

"Since you ladies are finished measuring your dicks, can we have some food?" Blue asked.

"Oh, more cheese," Brea said as she took the tray from Bernadette. "I love cheese."

"Girl, you are drunk," Blue said as she watched Brea's hand hover over the tray as she decided which piece to eat first.

"Have you ever had a dream about cheese?" Matalie asked.

"Oh shit. Try this one. *It's* a dream," Brea said as she held the tray out toward me.

"Sweet dreams are made of cheese," Matalie sang. *"Who am I to . . ."*

When Matalie faltered, trying to make up more lyrics, Blue chimed in, *"Who am I to dis a Brie?"*

"Get it?" Pandora cackled. "A Brie? Like our Brea?"

"Traveled the world and the seven seas . . ." I heard Hammer start in from somewhere behind us, and then he let out an 'oomph' when someone hit him.

"Here comes the cavalry," Bernadette said as she twisted around in her chair to look for Stamp. I turned around, too, and watched the men file into the room and split off toward their women. When she finally caught sight of him, she whispered, "Damn, he's hot."

"You know, the people that were working here today are going to be talking about us for days. Maybe even months," I said as I stood so I could greet Boss with a kiss.

"I'm sure it's not often that they're invaded by a bunch of women who get drunk and roll around on the floor."

I laughed at Frankie as I walked into Boss's arms. "Hey, handsome. Fancy meeting you here."

"Did you have fun with your girls?"

I nodded before I tiptoed up for a kiss. "You know it's always an adventure when we get together, no matter where we end up."

"That's exactly what scares me, Cool Cat."

5

PREACHER

"Where exactly are we going today?" I asked after I'd kissed Blue goodbye and joined the guys downstairs.

"Anywhere but that planning meeting they've got going on, and we've got to go try on our suits and tuxedos," Bug said as he nodded at the doorman.

"They're not really planning anything," Santa admitted. "Frankie just got them all together by saying that. She's gonna butter them up and make them go shopping."

I couldn't help but laugh at the devious look Santa shot me as he got into the Town Car. As I crawled in behind him, I said, "You mean butter your sister up so *she'll* go shopping."

"Brea's not all that into it either," Chef admitted.

Bug shook his head and sighed. "Maylee thinks it's an Olympic sport."

"I'm pretty sure my old lady would take home a gold medal if it was," Santa said with a knowing look.

"Matalie has her days," Captain agreed. "Especially when it comes to shoes or shit for the grandkids."

"My girls can spend *hours* shopping and come home

with two fucking bags. You'd think they'd have a little more to show for all that effort."

Boss's bark of laughter interrupted Kitty before he said, "You *want* them to spend more money?"

"Hell no, I just don't know what the fuck they're doing at the mall for so long when all they come home with is one or two things."

"Son, I'm not sure how to tell you this, but they're not at the mall to shop," Hammer said earnestly.

"Then what the fuck are they doing there for hours?"

"Kitty, there comes a time in a young man's life when he realizes the best place to pick up girls is at the mall," Hook explained with a grimace. "So if the girls are at the mall for hours and there are boys at the mall for hours . . ."

"They go to the mall to see boys?" Kitty asked, the horror obvious on his face.

"And now the blinders have fallen away," Hammer said sadly.

"I'm gonna say it now, Kitty. Gizmo's already got a lot going on and looking like a creeper at the mall every Saturday is not even on the horizon for him," Boss said firmly. "You're gonna have to trust they'll make good decisions and that the boys . . ."

"Were you *ever* a teenage boy, or did you morph from toddler to grumpy old man?" I asked. "Boys that age don't make decisions with their brains, and I don't believe girls do either. Teenage decision making is what put me in prison."

"Preach it, brother," Santa said with a grin. "It's not what put me in prison, but it sure as hell got me into a world of trouble before I ended up there."

"I need a drink," Kitty mumbled as he slumped down in his seat. "Where are we going again?"

"To have a drink," Stamp said with a laugh. "And to meet up with one of my own teenage decisions to look at jewelry."

"Jewelry?" I asked.

"I'm gonna propose to Paula. Frankie and Bernadette gave me some ideas to make it memorable," Hook told us. The car erupted into cheers and congratulations, and then he smiled nervously. "I'm not sure if she's gonna get happy tears and say yes or stab me for fucking with the status quo."

I winced. "It could go either way with that one."

"Are you ever gonna make an honest woman out of my sister or what?" Santa asked.

Captain started laughing. "It would take more than a fucking ring for that!" I glared at him for a second, and he grinned at me. "It had to be said, man."

"She'd run for the hills. I got her to promise me forever, and I've got no illusions there'll be a real preacher in our future anytime soon."

"But she gave you a date, right?" Santa asked. "She's always had a specific date in mind for her own wedding."

"If she's got a date, then what's the problem?" Hammer asked.

"She said she'll only get married on February 30th."

Hammer barked out a laugh. "Shit. She's good."

"Yeah," I grumbled. I took a deep breath, knowing I'd wear her down someday and smiled at my friend. "So you've got a plan, huh? Anything we can do?"

"Help me find her when she runs away?" Hook asked uncertainly.

I nodded, knowing the man was more than half-serious. "I'll put trackers on her again."

"I can help with that," Hammer assured us.

"We sound like a car full of psychos," I admitted with a chuckle.

The car we were in came to a stop on a busy street, and we started piling out. Once we'd regrouped on the sidewalk, Hook asked, "So what's so special about this place where we're going?"

"My boys own it. We're in their territory now," Stamp explained. "There's a woman inside who's gonna help Hook find the perfect ring."

When we got close enough, the door was opened by a burly man whose face lit up when he saw Stamp. He let the door go and grinned before he pulled him into a bear hug. "Valentine! It's good to see you, old friend."

"Carlo! It's been a while."

"The boys told us you were coming up for the wedding, but I had no idea you'd be here today."

"Guys, this is my old friend Carlo Robono," Stamp said. When he started to introduce all of us, Carlo waved him off and opened the door again. "Get in out of the cold. Let's go to the back room and get a drink. You can introduce your friends then."

Stamp nodded and walked into the store, and I followed a few steps behind him. It was a bright and airy shop with glass display cases placed strategically amid antiques and other pricey items. There was a stunningly beautiful woman standing behind the far counter, and when Stamp called out to her, she broke out into a huge smile.

"Valentine!" she said as she rushed around the counter. She motioned toward a woman standing off to the side, and she walked forward to take our coats. Once she had them piled in her arms, she disappeared through a door I hadn't noticed before.

The woman who had come out to greet Stamp stepped out of his arms before she smiled at us and said, "You must be Valentine's Texas family. It's a pleasure to meet all of you."

"Marla, Carlo, let me introduce you to the guys." He pointed at each of us, and I nodded and smiled after he said my name.

"Why don't the rest of you go with Carlo and get comfortable while I help . . . Hook, wasn't it?"

Hook nodded and smiled before he said, "Yes, ma'am."

Marla put her arm through his and started leading him away as she asked him to describe his 'one true love.'

"You're never gonna believe this, Marla, but Hook's true love is Paola Moretti," Stamp called out as they walked away. I saw Marla's mouth drop open as Carlo hissed, "What the fuck?" with a look of disbelief. Stamp shook his head as he laughed at their reactions. "It's a long story, man."

BUG

I slipped my phone into my pocket and told the guys, "I think we're gonna need to speed things up here, gentlemen. Our ladies are three sheets to the wind already, and Maylee's pretty sure they're not gonna last much longer."

"These two gentlemen are the last ones," Mario, the man who'd been in charge of everything since we walked into the exclusive store, said after he glanced down at his clipboard. "Would you like me to have William refill your drink once more?"

"Sure," I said as I lifted my rocks glass and took one last sip before Mario took it away.

"If more shopping trips included an open bar, we'd never bitch about going with our women," Boss said agreeably as he handed his glass to Mario.

"He's getting way too up close and personal for Preacher," Santa whispered as he watched our friend glare at the same man who'd measured me. "And I thought it was funny when they measured Boss."

"That wasn't fucking funny at all," Boss grumbled. "You could have warned me."

"Have you never watched *Friends?*" Hammer asked. Boss stared at him with his eyebrows raised in question and leaned forward as he slowly listed out the characters from the show. "None of that rings a bell?"

"That was one of the most unrealistic shows on television," Stamp scoffed. "Do you know how much an apartment the size of theirs would go for in the city? Seriously?"

"How much?"

"A two-bedroom in Greenwich goes for almost 10K a month," Stamp explained. "A personal shopper and a sous chef wouldn't be able to afford a closet in that building let alone a giant place like theirs."

"It was rent-controlled," Hammer argued. "It was originally one of their grandmother's."

"And the neighbor guys? Some mid-level computer guy and an actor who can't hold down a job?"

"I don't have any bright ideas about that one," Hammer conceded.

"He was a gigolo," I told them with a shrug. "Depending on his clientele, he could have easily covered the rent on that place."

"If you ruin that show for me, I will gut you right here in this fancy ass store," Santa grumbled. "Frankie already laughs about half the shit she sees on there, but I like it."

"I like it, too, I'm just being realistic," I argued.

"Maybe he had mob connections," Stamp suggested. "He *was* Italian."

"So was Chef Boyardee, and he wasn't in the mafia," Kitty slurred. "Fuck, I'm drunk. That came out before I realized how stupid it sounded."

"Maybe you should slow down since we're about to have to go babysit the ladies," Boss pointed out.

"We've got to take them through Central Park on the way back to the hotel," Santa told us. "Blue hates clowns, so I want to find a mime and see what happens."

I sighed. "Why do you pick on your sister?"

"Have you met her?"

"He just thinks it's funny to get her all riled up and then watch you have to calm her down," Boss said through his laughter. "It is pretty damn funny."

"Hammer picks on her too," Santa said with a shrug. Preacher glared at him, and Hammer grinned when Santa explained, "He fucks with you, gets you all riled up, and then she has to deal with it. It's fucking hilarious."

"It's like a two-for-one sale," Hammer said before he clinked his glass against Santa's. "You're welcome."

Captain stepped down from the platform in front of the mirrors where he'd been while the man fitted his tuxedo and walked toward the dressing room just as another tailor finished with Hook.

"Looks like it's about time to go, gentlemen," I noted as I took a big drink from my glass. "I'm ready to get back to my girl and my woman."

"I need to have a sit-down with Blue and explain why Hammer is now our mutual enemy," Preacher said as he finished the amber liquid in his glass. "You're screwed, buddy."

"Somehow, she scares me a little more than you do," Hammer admitted. "Really, all the women do."

"That's the smartest thing I've ever heard you say, brother," Boss said as he stood up and took his coat from the gentlemen who'd appeared from a side door. "They're especially terrifying when they've been drinking together."

Captain, having heard the tail end of our conversation, chimed in, "Matalie and I can't practice in the state of New York, so you are on your own if something happens."

"Nah," Stamp said as he reached for his coat. "We've got solid connections here. Since Matalie's as wild as the rest of them, you might need to keep that in mind."

"Noted," Captain said with a grin. "Let's go get our ladies. They've had a long day of shopping and champagne, and I believe they might just need some tender care and attention."

"To our ladies," I said as I held my glass aloft. I waited for the rest of the men who were still holding drinks to lift theirs before I said, "Let's hope the bubbly has done its job, we're going to get some hot, drunk, hotel sex and not go home with crushing debt."

6

AUGUST

"Do we really have to get out of bed?" Tyler asked as he pressed against my back. "I'd be content to stay here with you and watch the lights again."

"Our view from this room is stunning, isn't it? I'm not usually one for extravagance, but I could get used to this."

"I can guarantee I won't ever be able to afford this type of thing, Sweets. Hell, even if I could afford it, I'm not sure . . ."

"I looked online to find this room's rate, Tyler, and let me say that if you did lose your mind and rent a room like this, I would probably have to kill you."

Tyler laughed, and I felt the rumble of his chest against my back. "God, I love you."

"I love you too."

"You're aching to call them again, aren't you?"

"And you're not?" I asked as I reached for my phone on the nightstand. "We've gotta start getting ready for dinner in an hour, and they're gonna be . . ."

"Call them, Sweets. I miss them too."

I smiled at his admission, then hit the button to video chat with Mary so I could see the girls before she put them to bed.

It had been eight months since the first time I met my daughters, and even though there had been some rough patches adjusting to the change, I wouldn't trade a single minute. Since the girls came to live with us and Tyler was no longer killing himself trying to work all day and night with a million chores in between, the two of us had really enjoyed adjusting to married life and parenthood.

Together, we'd gotten through ear infections and stomach viruses and watched the girls blossom and explore their new home. They'd had a wonderful life with Carl and Mary, but since they'd come to live with us full-time, their worlds had expanded to include the Time Served families along with the Ares couples.

Blue hadn't lied when she said Luxe would be her little friend. They were inseparable when they were together. As a matter of fact, a week after Luxe started calling me 'Mama,' she said 'Blue' for the first time.

Blue had been beside herself and danced around the bonfire with Luxe in her arms as I soothed Tyler's hurt feelings. Shortly after, Luxe called out for 'Dada' after she'd fallen and bumped her head. I saw tears in Tyler's eyes as he took her from my arms. She'd laid her head against his chest, the place she felt most safe and comfortable, no matter what was going on around her.

"Hello, New Yorkers!" Mary said as our call connected. "How was your day out in the wilds of the big city?"

"It was awesome! We went to the Bronx zoo and then had lunch at a bistro Stamp's family owns. When we were finished there, the driver took us back to Central Park and we had a carriage ride."

"That sounds like a lot of fun! What are you doing tomorrow?"

"Frankie made arrangements for us to spend the day with Sis and Soda. We'll have a tour guide that's going to take us on a private boat to see the Statue of Liberty and Ellis Island."

"Wow. What's everyone else doing while y'all tour the town?"

"They're doing wedding stuff. They had to go to their dress fitting and get their shoes today," I explained. "Apparently, they went to a very bougie place and drank way too much champagne while they shopped. When we got here a few hours ago, we rode up in the elevator with some of them. Dad was giving Aunt Matalie a piggyback ride because she said she couldn't feel her feet, and Pandora was draped over Kitty's shoulder because she was out cold."

"Oh my," Mary said before she started laughing. "They must have had a great day."

"Yeah, right as the elevator doors closed on the scene in the lobby, I saw Blue and Brea sitting on a luggage trolley while Hammer spun it like a merry-go-round. Paula and Jenn were passed out on another cart while Boss and Hook waited on the next elevator so they could wheel them up to their rooms."

"Maylee, Frankie, and Bernadette were in much better shape and dragging their guys out shopping," I explained. "I'm pretty sure this hotel hasn't seen anything like our bunch before."

"I googled that place, and I think you may be right. I've certainly never been anywhere that elegant."

Tyler laughed and replied, "Mary, the only ones that have seen anything this fancy are Frankie, Paula, and Stamp because they grew up in this lifestyle and then Maylee because . . . well, because she's from Vegas."

I bit back a grin at Tyler's explanation of Maylee's previous life, which I'd heard stories about, and watched as Mary walked out to her sunroom. I could hear a television in the background playing Luxe's favorite show and the twins chattering and squealing at one another. The sound of the television disappeared just a few seconds after Mary turned the camera around so we could see the girls.

"Say something," Mary whispered.

"Hey, cuties," Tyler said with a grin as he scooted closer to the phone screen. I lifted my head so he could put his arm under it as we watched the girls get excited at the sound of his voice. "How are my girls?"

"Dada! Dada!" Luxe squealed as she got to her feet and wobbled toward the camera. Mary turned the view around again after she sat down on the couch, and we watched Luxe come into the frame as she grabbed for the phone.

"Hi, sweetheart!" I said to my grinning daughter. "Are you having fun?"

Luxe chattered at the screen and then tried to pull the phone out of Mary's hand, probably so she could put it in her mouth. Mary rescued the phone and turned the view around so we could see the twins crawling toward her.

"They've had a pretty exciting day. We spent the morning in the garden, then had macaroni and cheese before their naps. Carl brought home a wading pool for them and set it up while they were sleeping so the water could get warm. They spent almost two hours splashing around before we came inside."

"Oh, I miss them so much," I whispered as tears filled my eyes. Tyler squeezed me closer to him and started talking to Mary as I watched our girls playing happily. They'd lost interest with the call, which broke my heart but made me happy at the same time, knowing they were content where they were. Finally, Mary said she had to go, and Tyler and I said our goodbyes, blowing kisses at the girls before we disconnected. As I let the phone drop onto my chest, I said, "I think they've gotten bigger."

"It's only been a few days, Sweets."

"I miss them."

"I do too. Want me to take your mind off of your worries?" Tyler asked as he pulled his arm out from under my head and got up on his hands and knees so he was towering above me. "I can."

"We're going to have to get ready in just a few minutes."

"I'll make it quick but mind-blowing," Tyler promised as he stretched out on top of my body, his already hard cock already hard and nestling between my legs, just inches from where it needed to be. "Tonight, when we're finished downstairs, we can christen our balcony."

"Oh, I can't wait," I purred as Tyler nibbled on my

neck.

I jumped and Tyler stilled when someone thumped on the door of our hotel room. I heard my dad's voice warn, "One hour until we have to be downstairs!"

Tyler called out an acknowledgement and then reached down to rub his cock around my clit as he asked, "How long will it take you to get ready?"

"Twenty minutes, tops," I gasped. When Tyler pushed his cock deep in one thrust, I changed my mind. "Actually, I shouldn't take more than 10."

"In that case, we've got plenty of time."

PANDORA

"Mom! Wake up!" Hadley squealed as she threw herself into bed beside me.

"I woke up when you girls walked into our suite," I grumbled as I pulled the pillow out from under my head to cover my face. "Why are you so loud? You're going to wake up your brother."

"Kitty took him to the park with Bug and Boo," Harper explained. "We saw them in the lobby."

I stretched my arms above my head and then lifted the pillow to study my girls. "Did y'all have fun today?"

"We had *the best* time!" Hannah said as she draped her body over my legs and propped her head on her hand. "We're going exploring again tomorrow, and then we're going to meet everyone in the park to go ice skating."

"Everyone?"

"Yeah! The itinerary was attached to Bernadette's email."

"Bernadette sent an email?"

"Duh," Hadley said with an eye roll. When I glared at her, she grinned and continued, "You're usually a little more with it than that."

"I spent more than half the day with her. You'd think she'd have mentioned an itinerary."

"I think you're grumpy because you don't want to go skating," Harper ribbed. "I'm excited!"

"And I'm excited for you," I said as I sat up in bed. I put my hands over my face and took a few deep breaths as I waited for the room to stop spinning. "Good grief. This week is going to kill me."

"You're still drunk, aren't you?" Hannah asked.

"What makes you think I drank today?" I hedged as I wondered how in the hell we'd gotten back to the hotel. The last thing I remembered was taking a swig of champagne straight from the bottle as we were hugging our new friend, Anna. I'd made Kitty give her one of my cards so we could stay in touch and the rest is a mystery.

"We were here when you came back from your *dress*

fitting," Hannah said with air quotes. "We saw Kitty carrying you through the lobby to the elevator like a sack of potatoes."

"Oh. Well . . ."

"And then Blue threw up and sprayed it all over the place because Hammer was spinning her and Brea in circles," Hadley explained. She shuddered and took a deep breath through her nose before she described, "It was a lot like *The Exorcist,* but her head didn't spin."

"Shit," I whispered, imagining how *that* went over in the lobby of a place like this. I could see the whole thing happening in slow motion, and I felt my stomach flip. "That sounds . . . God . . . It's just . . ."

"She's gonna blow!" Hannah said as she scrambled off the bed.

Someone thrust an ice bucket at me, and I took it just as I gagged and threw up at least half a gallon of champagne and what looked like a . . . hot dog.

"Oh man! That's nasty," Hadley said right before she gagged.

"When did I eat a hot dog?" I asked as I wiped my mouth on the back of my hand. "What the hell?"

I got up and stumbled to the bathroom. After I'd dumped and washed the ice bucket, I brushed my teeth and then got into the shower. While I stood there under the hot spray, images of what we'd done after we left the bridal shop came to me in flashes, and I couldn't help but laugh.

We'd walked through Central Park with the guys,

laughing as Blue, Preacher, and Brea stayed alert for muggers and then stopped to listen to a man playing a violin. Not far away were some street performers dancing to music coming from a speaker they had, and somehow, they ended up in front of the violinist with us. After he switched from current hits to classic country, we tried to teach the dancers how to two-step and do the Cotton-Eyed Joe.

The last thing I remember was watching Marler hand a wad of bills to one of the dancers, and then I woke up hearing the kids giggling and carrying on as they came into the suite.

I leaned forward and rested my forehead on the cool tile as I wondered if my liver would make it back to Texas unscathed. Considering we had lunches and dinner parties scheduled for the next three days as well as a bridal shower, a lingerie party, *and* a bachelorette party, I wasn't sure I'd make it through the wedding, let alone the reception and the trip home.

"I'm back," I heard Marler say from right outside the shower. I opened the glass door a fraction to say something to him, and he started laughing. "How ya feeling, sweetheart?"

"I think I'm still a little drunk," I admitted.

Marler snickered and handed me a bottle of Gatorade before he reached into his pocket and pulled out a few pills. "Tylenol for the impending headache, and Gatorade to stave off the dehydration from trying to pickle your liver. Hopefully those will do the trick because we've got dinner in less than an hour."

"Where's Jared?"

"Desi and Lyric took him and Boo to the penthouse. We can pick him up when we're finished."

"I'm a horrible mother," I moaned before I swallowed the pills with a few chugs of the drink Marler had handed me. When it was half gone, I was already feeling better, and I handed it back to him. "Do you think I'm a horrible mother?"

"Of course not," Marler said with his eyebrows knitted together. "Why would you even ask that?"

"The girls know I was drunk this afternoon."

"Honey, *everyone* knows y'all were drunk this afternoon."

"That's not a good example to set. Think of what they're learning from me," I wailed.

"When you start teaching them how to cut lines on your makeup mirror using a credit card you *borrowed* from your elderly neighbor, then I'll say you're not a good example. Right now, you're just a word of warning that even occasional binge drinking is bad and can make people puke in lobbies and toss their cookies into ice buckets."

"The credit card and coke on the mirror was oddly specific," I muttered before I shut the shower door and leaned back into the water. Loud enough that he could hear me, I said, "I know you won't let me get that far."

"I know you'd never steal from the elderly, babe," Marler assured me before he laughed again. "You better hurry up. The girls are almost ready, and I will be, too, as soon as I change clothes."

"Ten more minutes!"

"Three," Marler bartered.

"Eight!"

"Five, and if you're not out when time's up, I'm going to show your daughters the video I took of you and Matalie harassing that mime in Central Park."

"What?"

"Hurry up, Pandora! Clock's ticking!"

7

MATALIE

"Nope!" Gus said as I walked out of the bedroom and into the living area of our suite.

I stopped in my tracks and smoothed my hands down over my hips as I looked down at the blouse I was wearing. "You don't like it?"

I could tell that the opposite was the case by the predatory look in his eyes as he stood up and stalked toward me. I put my hands up to ward him off as I shook my head. "No! We're going to be late if . . ."

"I promise to make it good for you."

"No, sir!" I said as I sprinted toward the door.

"I'll make it quick."

"Absolutely not," I yelled as Gus molded himself to my back and pressed me against the door. "I took forever doing my hair and makeup, and you're not going to ruin . . ."

Gus nibbled on my neck and whispered, "I could take you just like this, and your makeup would be fine."

He snaked his arms around me and cupped my breasts, and without thought, I pressed my ass against him. "You'll wrinkle my skirt."

Gus nudged the crack of my ass with his cock and whispered, "Do you really care about the skirt, Matalie?"

The second he nipped at my neck with his teeth, the thought of wrinkles slipped out of my mind completely.

"I think I knew this would happen," I mumbled as I felt Gus's hands tugging up the skirt I'd chosen for tonight. Inch by maddening inch, he exposed my legs until finally I heard him let out a long breath. "I knew you'd like those."

"You were going to wear these all night and not tell me?" Gus asked as he pulled me away from the door and turned us so that we were walking toward the dining table near the wall of windows. "That's just cruel, Matalie."

"I was going to tell you while we ate dinner," I said, giving up my plans to tease him as the front of my thighs hit the table's edge.

"And when was I going to find out about this?" Gus said as pushed my upper body forward with one hand and cupped my naked sex with the other.

"When we snuck away from dinner to get busy somewhere."

"Is that what you'd rather?" Gus asked as he notched himself at my entrance and pushed in just enough to tease me. "Or," he said as he pushed his cock in a little deeper, "do you want to do this?" With a growl, I shoved my hips back to meet his and then collapsed when he laughed. "I might make you wait." I looked over my shoulder and glared as I squeezed my muscles around him, then smiled when a dreamy expression came across his face.

"You're gonna be the death of me," Gus murmured as he started to move.

With a wicked smile, I closed my eyes and focused on how the man I loved made me feel every time we were together like this. As he reached around to touch my clit, I turned my head so he could nibble and bite on my neck just the way I loved.

"But what a way to go, right?" I asked, knowing he might not even be able to hear me over the sound of our bodies coming together. I sucked in a ragged breath as I felt myself tightening, already on the verge of orgasm. When I let myself go, he was right behind me, growling in my ear as my body clutched at his.

When we were finally sated and breathless, I fell forward onto the table and sighed when his cock slipped out of me. I held myself still as he went to the bathroom and got a warm, wet washcloth and then I let him clean me up before I stood and adjusted my skirt that was now wrinkled.

"See, baby? We're not going to be too late after all," Gus said as he tried to help me smooth the wrinkles.

"I'm not sure if you're trying to help or if you want to just keep touching my ass," I said with a laugh before I moved toward the bathroom to look myself over one last time.

"Can't it be both?" Gus asked as he leaned against the doorframe and watched me touch up my lipstick. As he held my eyes in the mirror, he said, "Every day, I thank my lucky stars to have you in my life, Matalie."

"And I'm thankful for you too," I replied as I stepped into his arms. When I tipped my head back to look at him, I saw his pupils flare and felt him start to harden at my hip. I smiled seductively for a second before I shook my head in exasperation. "Why not? We're already late."

FRANKIE

"Francesca! You look stunning, my dear," my great-aunt Madallena said in Italian with a wicked gleam in her eye. "And the man you've chosen is just . . . delectable."

Isabetta, my other great-aunt, this one a little more staid and proper, gasped and then frowned at her sister before she said, "Behave!"

Madallena winked at me before she glanced at Christopher, who was standing beside me, before she said, "He can't understand us, Isabetta. Let an old lady say what's on her mind."

"He truly doesn't understand?" Isabetta asked.

I smiled as I slowly shook my head. "He might be able to pick up a word here and there because he knows some Spanish, but I doubt it." Just in case he *could* understand a few words, I decided it would be best to send him to mingle with his friends. I tiptoed up and gave him a kiss on the cheek before I asked in English, "Why don't you go hang out with the guys for a few minutes while I talk to my aunts?"

"Sure, Big City," Christopher said before he gently shook Isabetta's hand and then Madallena's. He gave them his sexiest grin, complete with those disarming dimples, and in flawless Italian, said, "It was a pleasure to meet you both. I see now where my love got her beauty and charm."

When the three of us stared at him in shock, Christopher winked at me and grinned. "Surprise!"

"How in the world . . ." I sputtered.

"That audiobook series I've been addicted to was really a language app," Christopher said in English before he leaned over and gave me a kiss that was hot enough to curl my toes. Then, in the guise of a hug, he whispered in my ear, "I wanted to know what you're saying when you come apart in my arms."

"You devil," I whispered as he walked off. He turned his head to look back at me, and with another wink, blew me a kiss.

"I bet he's a handful," Madallena said under her breath as we watched him join Boss, Preacher, and Hook on the other side of the room where they were talking to my brother, Federico. "Are all the men in Texas this . . . rough and wild?"

I heard Isabetta sigh as she brought her hand up to fiddle with the string of pearls I'd never seen her without. "They're so polite and charming, but I can sense danger in them."

"Exactly," Madallena whispered. "That's the sexiest part."

"Not *all* the men in Texas look like them, I just somehow managed to surround myself with some that are exceptionally handsome," I said as I motioned toward the doorway where Captain was walking in with Matalie, August, and Rodeo. "You should see them at home when they're comfortable. It's quite a sight."

"I seem to recognize that one from somewhere," Isabetta said as she studied Rodeo, who was escorting August with his hand on her lower back. "Is he a model? I believe I've seen him in a magazine. Possibly an advertisement?"

I had just taken a sip of my champagne, and the bubbles burned my nose when I started choking. I thought I was going to be okay until Madallena tilted her head and said, "I seem to remember him shirtless for some reason."

I was still trying to catch my breath from my coughing fit when my aunts wandered off to talk to one of my cousins. Jenn, Blue, and Brea walked up and looked at me curiously until I was finally able to gasp out, "I choked on my champagne."

"Sip, don't chug," Blue reprimanded. "We've still got a few hours of this, right? I've been taking it slow because I think I might still be drunk from this afternoon."

"Might?" Jenn asked.

"You look fresh and clean," I teased Brea as I grinned at her and Blue. "I heard about the exciting ride you got in the lobby."

"I am so glad I missed that," Jenn said with an exaggerated shudder. "I was napping."

"You were passed out with your head resting on Paula's boobs," Blue snapped. "I have pictures."

"I have video," I said as I gave my friends an innocent smile. "I asked the concierge to email it to me."

"Oh fuck off," Blue muttered as she looked around the room. "I need you to give me the scoop on all these people. Some of them look perfectly normal, but others have that dangerous vibe."

"Well, the guys are talking to my oldest brother, Federico, but you've met him already. Maylee and Bug are talking to Ziggy and Aurelio, my other brothers."

"Did you notice that Maylee was the one to introduce Ziggy to Bug?" Jenn asked.

"That doesn't surprise me. Ziggy travels to Vegas a lot to check on the family's properties."

"I wonder if . . ." Blue started to say something, but when she saw the look of disgust on my face, she immediately stopped talking.

"I recognize Stamp's boys, but who are the guys they're talking to?" Brea asked.

"Those are Stamp's nephews, Dante Jr. and Principe Jr. Their fathers were killed some years ago by Paula's dad."

"Whoa," Blue whispered.

"The two older men with them are Salvador Jr. and Bastiano Moretti. Their father is the man Stamp went to prison for killing in Dallas."

"Holy shit," Jenn hissed as she looked at me with wide eyes. "And they're all just hanging out in the same room?"

"Their father was a soulless bastard," I said simply. "It wasn't much of a loss on their part, believe me."

"But still . . . They're just gonna sit down to dinner with all that bad blood between them?" Blue asked.

"They're in business together now," I answered with a shrug. "Things have changed since Stamp, Paula, and I left home. If this were my wedding 20 years ago, there would have already been bloodshed."

"They all just get along like nothing happened?" Brea asked in shock.

"For decades, the four families spent most of their time and money trying to one-up each other. They kidnapped women, killed men, married for convenience, torched neighborhoods, and ruined countless lives in the war between the families. But our ancestors made one huge mistake."

"What's that?"

"They assumed their hatred of each other was vehement enough to rub off on their children, but when we were all sent to the same schools and grew up with each other, we learned that our parents had been thrown into horrible situations by their own families just like we were. And yet, they weren't any happier about their lot in life than the rest of us who'd lost so much."

"And you and Paula became friends," Jenn said in shock.

"I was raised to hate her, but half of the time, our families were allied. She and I were close enough that when things went south between the grown-ups, we just ignored it. Some of the others did the same thing. Turns out that the friends who treat you like family become the ones you trust more than the family that treats you like a pawn in some stupid game."

"It's horrible that you were made to feel that way, but I'm so glad you found each other."

"Paula's brothers were able to show her son a different way despite her dad and husband's influence, and then Zach started school with Stamp's twins. Vincente and Antonio sent their sons to the same school and encouraged their boys to befriend my brothers. Now they're making history by working together."

"And that's why it's so important that you have this blowout wedding here? To show everyone that you're friends now?" Blue asked.

"It's to show everyone that we're *family* now. A Russo is going to stand with Christopher at my wedding, and a Moretti with blood ties to the Campanas is going to be standing with me. All four families will be officially tied together in front of the world. *That* is why we're all here together."

"Holy shit," Blue whispered.

Jenn was just as awestruck. "I feel like we're on an episode of *The Sopranos* or something."

"Honey, the reality is so much grittier than what they can show on television," I said sincerely, remembering all the vendettas I'd seen carried out and the bloodshed I'd witnessed with my own eyes. "But they've all come together for a changing of the guard. Paula's brothers are now going to take a step back and be more of a balancing influence that ties the history to the present."

"They're willfully stepping down?" Jenn asked. "I didn't even know you could do that."

"Generally, you can't, but they're trying something new. They've already made the changes, and believe me when I tell you there are some that aren't happy about it. But with the new pact in place between the families, they've been able to slowly, meticulously sort out the ones that make the most waves. It's not going to go so peacefully when Vincente and Antonio make their announcement, but they're prepared for that."

"Is that why we have to have guards while we're out and about?" Blue asked.

"That's part of it. People in power don't like to lose that power, and they'll do whatever they have to do to keep it."

"Including hurting you or Paula?" Brea asked. As if she knew I was thinking about her, Bernadette's laugh floated across the expansive room and made us look over to where she was standing with Stamp's arm resting across her shoulders. "Oh shit. Bernadette's part of it now, too, huh?"

"She is," I confirmed.

"Is that why she's planning the wedding?" Brea asked.

"She's actually enjoying it," I replied. "She wants to open her own wedding and party planning business, and this is her trial run."

"If she can plan a shindig like this, then the people of Tenillo won't know what hit them," Blue said with a bark of laughter.

"With this wedding under her belt, the state of Texas won't know what hit it. She's going to have one hell of a reference, complete with pictures taken by all sorts of news outlets and websites," I assured them. "Believe me, Bernadette's about to become an overnight sensation among wealthy brides all over the US, not just Tenillo."

"I guess that's one way to get your business off the ground," Jenn said with a smile.

"As long as there's no violence on my wedding day, I think she'll be set," I joked. When the women looked at me with wide eyes, I shrugged. "Hey, a girl can dream, right?"

8

BERNADETTE

"How's my favorite stepmonster?" Matteo asked as he slid into the chair Valentine had just vacated. Luca, Matteo's twin, sat on my other side and smiled when I looked his way. "Are you enjoying all this family time?"

"Sure," I told him. "I haven't seen the two of you very much since we got here. How are you?"

Luca replied, "We're busy, but that's nothing new."

"Thank you for agreeing to check in on my house," I told them. "I was thinking about selling it when the renters put in their notice, but your dad convinced me to keep it."

"You should," Matteo said with a slow nod. "We'll take good care of it for you."

"I contacted the leasing agency you recommended and asked if there's a contract I need to sign, but they said you guys would take care of that too."

"We own the leasing agency," Luca explained. "Besides, if you sign a contract, then there will be reporting that has to be done and taxes that will need to be paid." He waved his hand dismissively and smiled that disarming smile that reminded me so much of his father. "This is a family thing, not a business thing, right?"

I couldn't help but wonder why it was so important to

keep my house off the radar, so to speak, but it didn't really matter to me. The house had been paid in full by my husband's life insurance payout after he died, so all I was liable for was taxes anyway. Any money that came in from renters was just extra in my pocket at the end of the month.

"This event business you want to open - is that only going to be in Texas, or can we use you occasionally too?"

I saw he was serious and had to ask, "Aren't there local companies you can use for your events?"

"Of course there are, but if you had a branch here, we'd definitely use your company every time."

"What kind of events are we talking about?"

"Weddings, dinners, parties, that sort of thing," Matteo explained as he leaned forward and rested his arms on the table. "If you need help staffing your office, I'm sure we can find people for you."

I wondered what sort of long game they were playing that might include a party planning business. It was evident that I needed to make a decision to either stay as far away from their plans as possible or go all in and help them with whatever their cover story might be.

Decision made, I sighed and said, "I suppose if I had a branch here, it would give me and your dad an excuse to visit more often, wouldn't it?"

"You don't ever need an excuse," Luca said with a frown marring his handsome face. "None of Dad's Tenillo family needs an excuse. We've already arranged to have a suite permanently reserved for you guys or anyone else who might want to visit."

"And, of course, Frankie and Santa will always have their own suite of rooms too," Matteo added.

"I suppose if I'm going to open a business here, I'll need to lease some office space," I mused, knowing they probably already had that covered too.

"There's a really nice building in Riverdale that might work. You and Dad should take a look at it before you leave."

I stared at Matteo for a few seconds before I asked, "Does he know you're going to use my business as a front, or is this all on you two?"

Completely ignoring my question as if neither had heard it, Luca said, "If you don't like the one in Riverdale, I'm sure we can find something else."

"I take it that's a no then."

"I think I might have the perfect office manager for you, if you're interested," Matteo offered.

"Oh really?"

"It's a girl that went to school with us," Matteo explained. "She's going through a nasty divorce and needs something to take her mind off things."

"Does she need a house to live in too?"

Matteo let his head drop forward and sighed. "She won't let me help her. Says my money is tainted. I thought since you need a renter and she needs a job, you might consider her."

"You've got a crush," I said in realization.

"It's more than a crush," Luca commented.

"Well, obviously if he's trying to find a house and job for her and being all shady while he does it." I smiled and told Matteo, "I think I'd like to meet this woman who's not wowed by all your money and power."

"She's not impressed *at all,*" Luca informed me before he grinned at his glaring brother. "It's kind of awesome."

"We're planning on staying for a few extra days after the wedding so I can reconnect with some old friends. If you figure out how to make this happen, I'll let your sweetheart rent my house *and* I'll interview her for a job."

"You are the best stepmom a guy could ever ask for," Matteo gushed.

Luca rolled his eyes, but I nudged him with my shoulder and then he smiled too. I leaned close to him and said, "I'm more than willing to help if there's some girl you're interested in too."

"I've got the world at my feet, Bernadette. There's no reason to attach a ball and chain just yet." Luca grinned and nudged me back before he said, "Besides, I've got way more charm than that one. I can take care of myself just fine."

"Why are you two over here flirting with my old lady?" Valentine asked as he walked toward our table.

"I was trying to convince her that she should go with a younger, more handsome Russo, but she's resistant," Luca teased. "I've got some time to work on her, though. You better watch out, old man."

"Don't let that devilish smile and wicked charm get to you, Birdie. These boys don't know how to handle a real woman yet," Valentine said with a mock glare directed toward his sons.

"Neither of them have a chance, Valentine. There's no way they can cook nearly as well as you."

"That's all he's got going for him?" Luca asked. "I'm not a slouch in the kitchen, you know. As a matter of fact . . ."

Valentine put his hand out for mine and said, "Birdie, get away from these little delinquents before they try to turn your head." I took his hand and stood up, and Valentine grinned. "See, boys? If you treat a woman right, she'll always be loyal."

"Well, I guess we'll see. They've convinced me to spend a day in Riverdale with them after the wedding," I explained. Valentine put his hand on my back and guided me toward a group of our friends milling about, ready for the dinner that was about to be served in the dining area right off the banquet room. "I'll let you know which way I'm leaning after that."

"Until then, I've got plenty of time to convince you that I'm the best Russo, don't I?" Valentine whispered close to my ear. "As a matter of fact, there's a room down the hall that might be the perfect place to get started."

"We'll miss dinner."

"I'll eat *you* for dinner and make sure we're back in

time for dessert."

"Lead the way, handsome."

BLUE

"I feel like that big marshmallow guy in the movies," Jude said as he zipped up the coat I'd bought him at the ski store.

"She came home with this thing and I thought, there's no fucking way it's that cold up there," Captain said as he pulled on a pair of gloves. "Then we stepped off the plane, and I started looking for fucking polar bears."

"Look at me," Matalie said before she did a dramatic spin and struck a pose. The red coat swirled around her, and she grinned as she flipped the houndstooth scarf over her shoulder. "I don't think I'm ever going to give this back to Maylee."

"You look so fancy," Frankie said as she and my brother joined us. "Is that coat okay, Blue?"

"It's perfect," I said as I smoothed my hand over the front of the wool peacoat I'd borrowed when we got to New York.

"Good color," Brea said as she walked up wearing a coat similar to the one I had on but in a burnt orange rather than midnight blue like mine. "When Frankie said she had all the winter stuff we'd need, I thought she might be exaggerating, but it was like walking into a department store."

"I've been collecting some of those pieces since I was a teenager," Frankie admitted. She turned to face my brother and ran her hands up his chest and over the coat she'd chosen for him before she tipped her face up for a kiss. "I'm slowly working on expanding Christopher's wardrobe too."

"Is he going to branch out and start wearing shirts with buttons?" I asked snidely. "I'm just afraid Frankie's going to lose patience and give up on my brother if he can't figure out how to dress himself."

"You're such a hag," Christopher said with an eye roll. "Are we ready yet? Where are we going anyway?"

Jenn, Boss, Paula, and Hook walked up just then, bundled up for the cold weather. "Where are Bug and Maylee?"

"They're hanging out in their room with Boo tonight," Jenn explained.

"Likely excuse," Jude muttered. "Kitty's not coming either."

Brea added, "Sis and Soda are on a date, and August and Rodeo are out exploring on their own. They're going to meet up with us later."

"How much later?" Jude asked. "Are we planning on staying out all night or something?"

"We might have so much fun on the subway that we

ride all night long and watch the sun rise," Paula teased. She glanced over her shoulder and grinned at Bernadette and Stamp as they walked up and complimented her on the coat she was wearing. Finally, with a wave toward one of the men that had been following us around since we got to New York, Paula nodded and said, "Let's go, people."

"Like we need a keeper," Jude said under his breath as he put his hand on my back and nudged me ahead of him.

"It's not for us, babe," I whispered. "They're watching out for Paula, Bernadette, and Frankie."

"Wouldn't need this shit if we were in Texas," he replied. "Can't even walk around this town without security. If we were at home, *we'd* be the security."

"I know you'll keep me safe out here in the big scary city," I assured Jude, trying to stroke his ego and make him a little more comfortable about the adventure we had planned.

"You're not carrying a purse are you?" Jude asked right before he ran his hand over my ass. "Nothing in your pockets for someone to steal?"

"No one's going to pick my pockets, Jude. You're going to be right there with me the whole time."

"Stay close to me. You never know what might happen in a city this size. There's always stuff on the news, and they've got all those crazy murderers running loose . . ." When I raised my eyebrows and looked at him in question, he shrugged. "I just worry about your safety, Blue."

"Letting these women out in the wild, untamed city is probably gonna get us all on the morning news," Chef agreed.

"Did they tell you that they want to witness a mugging? And then what do they plan to do when they catch the guy?"

"Why would you . . ." Jude shook his head and sighed. "I don't even want to know, do I?"

I bit my lip as I slowly shook my head, and our friends laughed at the tortured look on Jude's face.

"Let's get this shit over and get everybody back here in one piece," Jude said as we all stopped on the street in front of the hotel.

"Love you, Jude," I said as I squeezed his hand through our gloves.

"I love you, too, woman, but you're gonna be the death of me. You know that, right?"

"Let's get cabs," I suggested.

"No," Frankie said firmly. "The car should be here any second now."

"My princess doesn't *do* cabs," Christopher said loudly. "The lady has standards."

"I just want to hail one and then get in a screaming match with the driver when he overcharges me," Brea said. When I nodded, she asked, "Wouldn't that be fun? I've seen that on *so* many movies and tv shows."

"I'm walkin' here!" Captain yelled in his best De Niro impression.

"How far are we going?" Jude asked as we followed Frankie and my brother with the rest of our friends.

"We didn't get to do it yesterday, so let's ride the subway tonight," Pandora suggested. I saw Frankie rub her forehead and realized Pandora had seen the same thing when she said, "Come on, Frankie. Don't be such a snob. We want the real experience."

"I want to get home to Texas in one piece," Jude grumbled. "Shooting through a tunnel in a soda can is not the way I want to die."

"You're not gonna die, Preacher," Boss assured him. "Where's Hammer?"

"He said he had plans," Chef answered. "I told him to text me when he gets finished. Maybe we can meet up."

"Where are we going exactly?" Boss asked as he watched Jenn climb into the van. Before anyone could answer, he climbed in after her, and we all followed suit. Once we were situated, he asked, "Why the secrecy? Where are we going?"

"We're going to have dessert," Frankie said with a huge smile. "There's a famous delicatessen that has the best milkshake you've ever tasted. It's almost orgasmic."

Paula threw her head back and laughed. "That's freaking awesome, Frankie. They're gonna love it."

"What are we doing tomorrow?" Brea asked.

"I sent all of you the itinerary," Bernadette chided. "Do you not read your email?"

"I'm on vacation."

"Blue, you're the worst at checking your messages

anyway. Don't even pretend to use this trip as an excuse."

"Wow. I didn't even see that bus coming before you threw me under it, Paula. Thanks." Paula smirked, and I couldn't resist flipping her off. "So . . . tomorrow?"

"We are having a pampering session at the club while the men golf," Bernadette said with a smile.

"Say again?" I asked at the same time as Jude, who was sitting next to me.

"We're golfing?" Santa asked.

Boss chuckled as he asked, "At a country club?"

"It's colder than a well digger's ass outside, and you want us to play golf?" Jude asked.

Frustrated now, Bernadette asked, "Did *anyone* read the email?"

"The temperature is supposed to be almost 60 degrees tomorrow and . . ."

"You know that's cold, right?" Captain asked Bernadette.

"There's no snow and the sun will be out," Frankie told them. "It's perfectly normal to play golf year-round."

"If you live in Florida!" Jude argued.

"Golf started in Scotland. It barely gets above 60 degrees there during the hottest part of the year," Bernadette argued.

"My brothers play all year," Frankie added.

"I didn't bring my golf shoes," Chef complained.

Brea winked at him before she said, "*I* read my email and packed them for you along with your clubs. They were in that tub I had Soda put in the truck."

Chef hooked his hand around the back of Brea's neck and pulled her toward him for a kiss right before he started mumbling something in her ear that made her eyes close and an excited smile come across her face.

"I'm gonna be drinkin'," Santa said grumpily.

"What's a pampering session?" Paula asked.

"You'll see," Bernadette said secretively. "It's going to be lots of fun, I promise."

The van we were in pulled to a stop at the curb. "Frankie, I'm still full from dinner."

"Trust me," Frankie replied before Santa opened the door and stepped onto the sidewalk, turning around to hold his hand out for Frankie. I could see the security guard in the passenger seat let out a tortured sigh, and it took everything I had not to laugh.

"Do you want some dessert, Jude?" I asked as we waited on the others in front of us to climb out.

"What I want isn't served here," Jude said in a low voice so only I could hear. "If I eat what I want for dessert at this place, we'll both get arrested."

"I've created a monster."

"And monsters have an insatiable appetite."

PAULA

"So is that milkshake *orgasmic?*" I asked my friends before I took another bite of my own.

"Close," Maylee said.

Jenn, Brea, and Blue didn't say anything but nodded. Pandora asked, "Why do the two of you keep saying orgasmic like it's something important?"

"This deli is famous for a classic movie scene," I hinted. All eyes turned to me as Frankie and Bernadette grinned.

After a few seconds, they all started looking around the deli, but Jenn was the first person to figure it out. Blue was right behind her. I knew they had realized what movie I was talking about when they threw their heads back and had very loud, very realistic fake orgasms, sitting right there at the table with all the guys, surrounded by strangers.

"What. In. The. Fuck?" Preacher hissed as he stared at Blue like she was crazy.

Boss frowned. "That is *not* what you sound like."

"That's a scene from the movie *When Harry Met Sally,*" Jenn explained. "Billy Crystal says that he'd know if a woman was faking her orgasm so she fakes one right there in the middle of the diner to prove him wrong."

"Women can just turn it on and off like that?" Preacher asked.

"Oh honey," Blue said as she reached out and rested her hand on Preacher's cheek. "I can honestly say I've never done that with *you*."

Boss was staring at Jenn and Captain was studying Matalie's face when Hook leaned over and said, "Let me hear what a fake one sounds like."

"You might already know," I retorted. Hook immediately scowled, and I couldn't help but laugh. "I'm just kidding. You know I enjoy it every time."

"There was that one time when . . ."

"I had a lot on my mind and you put in a good effort," I reassured him. "At least I didn't fake it, right?"

"How often do women do that?" Preacher asked.

"You mean other women besides the ones at the table who I am *sure* have never?" I asked.

"Man, I wish Maylee were here for this conversation," Blue said with a laugh. "She'd probably have a statistic or two."

"I think we should change the subject," Matalie suggested. Captain stared at her with wide eyes, and she shrugged before she reassured him, "For their benefit. I've got nothing to hide, Gus."

"So!" Frankie said cheerfully. "Who wants to . . ."

"Do it again," Preacher insisted just as Chef told Brea,

"You do one."

"I want to hear what your fake one sounds like," Santa told Frankie.

"But you know what mine sounds like," Frankie said without skipping a beat. When Santa's face dropped, Frankie specified, "The real one! You know what the real one sounds like! I've never faked it. With you. I've never faked it with you!"

Just to rescue my friend, I ran my hand over my throat and then grabbed my hair on the side of my head before I moaned loudly. Blue chimed in with a moan, right before Brea did the same. Jenn started in, too, and then Matalie added one of her own. Finally, Frankie joined us, and we did our best to tear the roof off the place with our breathy moans and fake exclamations.

"Excuse me," an older woman at a table nearby said after we'd let our shenanigans die down. I glanced over at the smiling lady and watched her stop the waitress who was walking past only to say, "I'll have what they're having."

The waitress rolled her eyes so hard I was sure it hurt. Everyone at our table roared with laughter along with the woman and her friend. Within the next minute, we struck up a conversation with the two and chatted while we finished our desserts.

"All of you came from Texas for a wedding?" the woman who'd introduced herself as Janna asked.

When we nodded, Matalie pointed at Frankie and Santa with her spoon and said, "They're getting hitched."

The next few minutes were spent discussing wedding plans, and I noticed that Lisa, Janna's friend, was studying Stamp. She finally asked, "Are you from *Russo's Road Trip*, by chance?"

Stamp nodded and the women got excited as they asked for a picture with him.

"It's so funny that they recognize him from TV and have no idea about his history or anything," Hook said as he leaned closer to me.

"Is it a closely guarded secret or something?" Jenn asked.

"If it is, it's not gonna be for long," Hook whispered. "From what the boys were saying, this shit's gonna at least make the local news."

"Oh, most definitely," I assured him. "And, if I had to guess, it will be an internet sensation by tomorrow morning."

"Why do you say that?" Jenn asked from beside me.

"Squeeze in so I can get everyone in the picture!" the waitress said as she took a step back. "Smile!"

I looked directly into the camera and smiled. We waited as she took a few more before she handed it back to Janna.

"I'm going to post this on all my pages! I'm so excited!" Lisa said as she bounced excitedly in her seat.

"She got a few thousand followers," Janna boasted. "I'd say she's a local celebrity."

"No," Lisa said humbly. "I'm not a celebrity by any means. I run a page about local history, and there's a lot of interest in that."

"Yep," I whispered to Jenn as Janna started typing in our names to tag us in her photo. "Shit's about to spread like wildfire."

"Because of Stamp? It might go viral because of his show."

"There's that," Frankie agreed with Jenn as she leaned closer to join our conversation. "But when the local history buffs following her see it, I assure you it's gonna blow up."

"Because of your families?"

"Because our friend Paula must have just risen from the dead."

"Oh shit," Jenn whispered.

"Zachary and my brothers as well as Frankie and her brothers have kept my secret for a long time, but we knew it would come to light when I came back for the wedding." Jenn looked shocked, but then her eyes got even wider when I said, "Earlier today, when I told the saleswoman my name was the first time I've introduced myself like that in *years*."

"How did it feel?"

I smiled before I took a deep, calming breath. "Terrifying and awesome at the same time."

MAYLEE

"How's Boo enjoying the new digs?" Blue asked as she sat next to me on the couch. "She's living the high life with a nanny in the penthouse and all the good stuff."

"She had a nanny in our Vegas penthouse, so this shouldn't be much of a change for her," I explained.

"I've always wondered about that," Blue pushed. "You went from living the high life in Vegas with fine restaurants and luxury shopping at your fingertips to Tenillo. There aren't any swanky restaurants or fancy places to shop, no bright lights or big city accommodations."

"Now that's my home," I said firmly. "It's Boo's home."

"Well, yeah," Blue said sarcastically. "I just thought it would be a sort of a culture shock for you."

"Over the years, I learned to become very adaptable. Besides, it's not like I moved from my penthouse to a shack in the swamp with no running water or AC."

"That sounds horrible," Blue admitted with a grimace. "Jude keeps saying he has property in a swamp somewhere and that we should go stay there for a few weeks. All I can imagine are mosquitos big enough to suck a pint at a time and gators that want payback for all the purses, shoes, and luggage that have been made out of their brethren."

I laughed at her description and lifted my foot to show her the light green Prada slingbacks I was wearing. "If there's ever an uprising, I should stay far away from anywhere crocodiles live." Movement outside the window caught my eye, and I asked, "What are they doing?"

Blue laughed. "It looks like they're teaching the New Yorkers how to shotgun a beer."

"Good grief," Brea said as she walked up behind the settee where we were sitting. "They haven't even made it to the first hole yet."

All of them - Boss, Hook, Chef, Preacher, Captain, Santa, Kitty, Rodeo, Stamp, Hammer, Soda, and, of course, Enzo were standing in a group that included Paula's son, Stamp's sons, Frankie's brothers, and several Ares Infidels. Each of them had a pocketknife in one hand and a beer in the other.

The men from New York were listening raptly to Hook's explanation and then watched as he demonstrated. Paula had walked up behind me at some point, and when Hook opened his mouth and thumped his chest, she sighed. "Look at my sweetheart, out there on the golf course at one of the most exclusive country clubs in the state, teaching my sweet child how to binge drink like a frat boy."

The rest of the men followed Hook's instructions, and even though a few of them weren't quite deft at the process, they all managed to get *most* of the beer in their mouth.

"It doesn't seem like that was Zachary's first attempt," I mused when Paula's son finished a split second before the rest of the men and held his empty can up with a laugh.

"He's an angel and a quick learner," Paula tried to bluff. Finally, she couldn't hold it in anymore and laughed as she said, "He won, though, so there's that!"

"Does anyone else find it strange that we're about to get massages and spa services in a room full of windows?" Brea asked.

Frankie, who had already changed into a plush robe the club supplied, walked over and sat between me and Blue before she answered, "I had them arrange it like this intentionally. With the way the building sits and how the ground slopes, we can see almost the entire course."

"So we get to watch golf? Yay," Paula said sarcastically.

"No, we get to watch *them* golf," Frankie said with laughter in her voice. "Bernadette arranged for each man to get a gift from Christopher just for today's event."

"What's that?" I asked.

"They each got a monogrammed flask full of 18-year-old Scotch that's going to help keep them warm," Frankie explained.

"That's nice," Jenn said as she walked up and joined us. "Oh look! They're going to make a toast."

The men held their flasks in front of them as Santa started speaking. Their faces were serious at first, but as he talked, they started smiling. Finally, they raised their flasks and took a drink.

We all laughed at the reaction of almost every man as the whisky burn took over and their faces morphed. A few of the men coughed, and I could tell that most of them were gasping for air.

"Not big Scotch fans, huh?" Jenn asked.

Frankie laughed. "Well, it's 80 proof, so that first sip was probably a little rough."

Paula giggled and then in a fake announcer's voice said, "And today's golf game is sponsored by really strong whisky with influences from the movies *Caddyshack* and *Happy Gilmore.*"

Frankie sighed and smiled before she said, "This is going to be awesome."

"Did your brothers have any idea what they were in for when they agreed to this?" I asked. "They're going to end up losing their membership by the time they're finished today."

Frankie patted my knee and shook her head. "No, they won't. They own this place, so the boys will be just fine cutting loose out there."

As the guys separated and got into carts, we watched other men we didn't recognize split up and follow along. "Some of those are caddies, but who are . . ." I noticed the video camera in one of the men's hands and gasped, "Are those men from the press?"

"No," Frankie giggled. "They're videographers I hired to document the day."

"Oh shit," Paula said as we all started laughing. "That's so great."

"Proof or it didn't happen," Jenn said through her laughter.

"I thought it would be fun to have some champagne and get pampered in this beautiful room while we watch the shitshow that's about to commence on the golf course."

"Frankie, my friend, you're a diabolical genius."

PANDORA

"What are they doing now?" I heard Frankie's muffled voice ask from the massage table behind us. She was facedown with a sheet covering her ass as the masseuse rubbed her legs. "Why am I even asking? I don't care."

"Boss is driving Bug, Captain is driving Hook, Stamp is driving Santa, Preacher is driving Hammer, and Marler is driving Ziggy," I explained.

"And?" Frankie called out.

"They're not really golfing. I think it's more like polo . . . sort of," Jenn explained from the chair next to mine. The woman giving her a pedicure asked a question, and Jenn nodded before she looked back up at the scene playing out in front of us and started giving Frankie and the other women who couldn't see the course a play-by-play. "One of the twins is surfing on top of the cart that Marler's driving, and it looks like . . . oh shit!"

My gaze snapped up from my manicure just in time to see the cart with Marler and Ziggy go barreling into the pond. One of Stamp's twins who had been riding on the top of the cart went flying into the water with a splash.

"Fuck!" Paula shouted, apparently watching the crash too. When the younger man stood up with his arms in the air like he was showing off his dismount for the Olympic judges, we all let out audible sighs of relief.

"He's gonna freeze his balls off," Blue said from behind me. I turned around and saw she was sitting on the edge of the massage table with her sheet wrapped around her, watching the course. "Are they just gonna sit there until the damn thing sinks or what?"

Just then, Marler and Ziggy bailed out of the cart and started wading toward the edge of the pond. I knew it wasn't that deep since Matteo was moving through waist-high water, but I imagined it was *really* cold.

"They're gonna get frostbite," Paula said as we watched their progress.

Two men with carts hurriedly drove to the pond where the guys were just coming out of the water. They handed them towels and blankets and then let them get into the golf carts to be brought back to the clubhouse.

"Prepare for an invasion," I warned the women. "I give it five minutes before we've got some really chilly company."

"Damn!" I heard a few of the women say at the same time.

I was right. Within just a few minutes, two of the three men appeared at the door, and one of the attendants walked them in to sit on the couch to my right. They were barefoot and wearing the same type of fluffy robes we all had on, and I noticed that they weren't exactly steady on their feet.

"Where's Enzo?" Maylee asked.

Ziggy, Frankie's brother, laughed and then cleared his throat, "He's still in . . ." He slurred his words, so he cleared his throat and tried again, this time speaking slowly. "He's sleeping on the sofa in the men's lounge."

"Well, shit," I heard Maylee mutter. "He's down for the count then, I'm sure."

Bernadette walked over to sit in the wingback chair near the couch. I heard her ask, "You're Matteo, right?" Apparently, she'd guessed correctly because she let out a little cheer before she asked, "Are you okay?"

"I'm all good," the younger man mumbled. "It's cold out there."

"Ziggy, I can't believe you guys wrecked a golf cart!" Frankie chastised from her massage table. She was clearly watching her brother's profile because she snapped, "Eyes front, man! Jeez!"

Ziggy giggled and leaned his head back on the couch. "The last time I drank like this was when we were kids."

"Are you referring to that time you stole a bottle of

Dad's Scotch, and we all ended up puking in the bushes?" Frankie asked.

"That was horrible," Paula moaned.

"Paola! My sweet love! I've been meaning to talk to you," Ziggy said cheerfully as he leaned forward to look around me to find Paula.

"Ziggy, I will get my naked ass up from this table and choke you to death," Frankie warned.

"I've been waiting for that woman my entire life," Ziggy protested. "Paula, I have been saving myself for you all these years, and I think . . ."

"Don't you have like 14 children and 9 ex-wives?" Paula interrupted.

"Well, not quite but . . ." Ziggy cleared his throat and then tried again. "Paula, I'd like to take you to dinner while you're in town. Now that you're out in the open again, I think it would be advan . . . advent . . . avante . . . Fuck."

"Advantageous?" I supplied.

"Yeah, that. It would be . . ." Ziggy leaned over the edge of the couch and stared at me earnestly before he loudly whispered, "Say it again."

"Advantageous."

". . . for us to get together. We should marry. Immediately." He cleared his throat and then shook his head as he blinked rapidly. He then added, "I'll make you my queen."

"Oh sweet Jesus," I heard Frankie grumble.

"And he's out," I said when his head fell back against the couch and he let out a loud snore. I looked over at Paula and realized she was blushing furiously. "Someone's got a crush."

"He's always had a thing for Paula," Frankie told us. "She broke his heart when she married that dumbass."

"Let's just keep that little conversation between us, shall we?" Paula suggested as she stared at Matteo. "Got that, youngster?"

"You know I'm not a kid, right?"

"Got that, *youngster?*" Paula said a little more forcefully.

"I don't even know what you're talking about right now."

"Good job," Bernadette said with a grin.

"I don't need Hook starting an international incident and getting me on the wrong side of things again," Paula admitted. "He's a pretty easy going guy but finding out another man proposed to me might irritate him a little."

"Just a tiny bit," Jenn agreed as she held her hand up with her fingers a millimeter apart.

"Once all of you leave, I'm going to give him mountains of shit about it. Just saying," Matteo slurred before he leaned his head back and closed his eyes. "I'm going to rest my eyes for a . . ."

"Another one bites the dust," Bernadette said with a grin before she got up and pulled a few lightweight blankets off a nearby cart. She covered each man and tucked the blankets around them before she stepped back and pulled her phone from her pocket. "I think I'll take a picture of this touching scene."

"I'm going to go check on Enzo," Maylee said as she stood up. She adjusted the tie on her robe and sighed. "God knows I owe him one after yesterday's shopping adventure."

"I think I'm going to cancel tonight's festivities," Frankie said as she walked around my chair with her purse in her hand.

"The ice skating or . . ."

Frankie interrupted Bernadette. "No, that's still on, but I'm sure they're going to be in no shape for a bachelor party, and I really don't think my liver could handle another drink."

"Do you think they'll be sober by the time we go skating?" Jenn asked.

Paula laughed wickedly before she said, "God, I hope not. That would be hilarious."

10

FRANKIE

"This is going to be a shitshow," Blue said as she laced up her skates.

"I'm so excited," Hannah said as she sat between me and Blue and bent over to take off her shoes.

"That's bullshit," Blue said with disgust as she watched Hadley plop down on the floor at our feet. Harper was next and sat on the floor beside her sister. "They can just drop to the ground like it's nothing. And just watch. They'll hop up like they're on a goddamn spring."

"There's no way I could sit down there without having help to get back up, and that's *without* having skates on," Jenn said as she stopped lacing her skates and watched the girls. "Look at how they just bend their legs in half like it's nothing."

"You can put your chin on your knee without any problem, can't you?" Paula asked.

All three girls rested their chins on their knees and laughed as we glared at them.

"I haven't been able to do that without help since . . . Fuck, I'm not sure I've ever been able to do that," Blue said with disgust.

"The boobs get in the way," Paula said with a sigh.

"All of this gets in the way," Blue said as she gestured towards her entire torso. "I bend over to tie my shoes and get winded."

"I cross my foot over my knee to tie my shoes," Brea explained as she was doing just that with her skate.

"I can do it," August said as she demonstrated the same pose the girls had taken.

Sis tried it and grinned before she sat up straight and shook her head. "I just crushed my boobs, but it was worth it just to see the looks on your faces."

"Why aren't all the guys ice skating?" Harper asked.

"Because they're smart enough to know that if they fall, it's gonna take weeks to recover," Matalie grumbled. "Why are we doing this again?"

"We can do this," Pandora cheered as she stood up. She carefully picked her way across the few feet from the bench to the wall, but when she tried to turn around, she wobbled and nearly fell. Once she was steady again, clinging to the partition, she winced and said, "Okay, so maybe we shouldn't do this."

"I've done this before, but I was younger," I admitted as I stood and balanced on my skates. "Oh, this is going to end badly."

The rest of my friends finished tying their skates and made their way over to the wall slowly where we stood, watching everyone on the ice.

"Look at those kids," Blue said as she motioned

toward the ice. "If they can do it, we can do it, right?"

A little girl in a bright blue coat was skating a few feet in front of her mom and squealed as she fell. She laughed as she tried to get back up, and we winced as the mom almost lost her balance trying to help her daughter.

"We're going in," Harper said as the girls walked toward the opening in the wall. August and Sis were right behind them, and I watched their progress wondering how close we were to the nearest hospital.

We tracked them as they slowly but surely started moving across the ice.

"I know it's horrible to wish something bad on your own children, but if they don't each fall at least once, I'm going to riot," Pandora grumbled.

As if the universe were on her side, all three girls squealed and then disappeared behind the wall as they fell together in a heap. August and Sis made their way back to try to help them get up and then they fell too.

"If that happens to me, I'm going to need to be put in traction," Brea mumbled as we leaned over the wall to watch the girls untangle themselves. "Of all the wild shit we've done together, this might be the most dangerous."

"At least the most dangerous physically," I agreed.

"I think our priorities are skewed," Maylee said with a sigh. "We were basically hostages in a broom closet, and we think *this* is scarier than that day."

"I'd rather be kidnapped and locked in an office

where I have to pee in a coffee cup again than do this," Paula said with a sigh.

"You peed in a coffee cup?" Pandora asked.

Paula looked at our friend and nodded. "I figured that if I did die, at least a little part of me would linger on for a while."

"I wonder what happened to that cup of pee after you were rescued," Blue said.

"The cops raided that place, so I'd assume someone found it," Brea told us. "There's probably some tech in the crime lab who's got a sample of your pee, trying to figure out where it fits in with the whole investigation."

"I was pretty fucked up after that shit with Julia. It took me forever to recover," Jenn said as she looked down at her hands. "I'm not really sure I'm willing to go out there and fuck up all those months of rehabilitation."

"I don't think you should risk it. If you fall, you're going to try to catch yourself. That's just natural," Brea said.

I sighed and noted, "If I hurt myself, I can't work."

"It hasn't been that long since I broke my hand either," Paula mused as we watched a woman fall close to the middle of the rink. We winced when she tried to get back up and fell again.

"Fuck, I feel old," Blue admitted sadly. "Back in the day, I'd dive right into something new without even thinking of the repercussions. Now I'm afraid of ice skating, of all things."

"I'm not doing it," Maylee said with a sigh. "I hurt my back getting the laundry out of the dryer last week, and I've got a baby to chase around."

"Look at the girls. I don't remember ever being quite that carefree," Pandora said as we watched her daughters laugh with Desi, Tanner, and Tyson, whose parents were members of the Ares Infidels, some of which were already out on the ice. The teenagers had been joined by some of the other young family members who had been escorting them around town. It obviously wasn't their first time on the ice. "It's probably a good thing Marler's not here."

"Who is that boy with his arm around Desi's waist?" Maylee asked.

"That's my nephew, Nicky. He's Freddie's oldest," I explained. "The twins are Ziggy's daughters, Ziva and Zara. The other two girls belong to my brother Aurelio."

"Come on! It's fun!" August said as she got closer to us.

Sis laughed and then wobbled. She took a second to steady herself and then stopped in front of us. "This is harder than I thought it would be, but I like it."

"Let's go around again," August suggested.

"Are we going out on the ice or not?" Blue asked as we watched August and Sis get farther away. "Fuck this. My feet already hurt. I'm changing back into my shoes."

"We've gotta do something fun tonight!" Matalie argued. "Come on! This is basically her bachelorette party, you guys."

"We're having her bachelorette party at a skating rink in the freezing ass cold? That's lame enough without adding injuries to that insult," Paula said firmly as she turned around and walked back over to our shoes.

"We've got to do something thrilling. Something wild," Brea suggested. "Something that doesn't make me feel ancient and . . . brittle."

"Like what?" I asked.

"If you say go to a club, I will have Blue punch you in the throat," Maylee warned as she sat down to change into her shoes.

"Why the hell do I have to do it?" Blue asked.

Maylee retorted, "I got a manicure today."

"So did I."

"Yes, but you don't really care what your nails look like," Maylee said sweetly.

"If I'm punching anyone, it's gonna be you."

"Blue, we don't hit our friends," Pandora chided.

"Ugh," Blue said with disgust in her voice. "Don't mom voice me. I'll punch you, too, just for that."

Brea waded in with her vote, "Come on, you guys! Let's go do something crazy. We're in New York City, for Christ's sake. We've got to have an adventure!"

"Well, the park was a dud. Not even one person tried to mug us," Blue complained.

"You guys watch way too much television," I complained. "I've never been mugged, and I grew up here."

"Same," Paula agreed with a nod.

"Because you walked around with security guards," Matalie clarified.

"Just once, I want to look at a mugger and say, *'That's not a knife.* This *is a knife.'* and then watch them run away in fear," Blue conceded. "Come on, ladies. Let's live a little."

"She needs to be committed for everyone's safety," I heard Bernadette mumble from somewhere beside me.

"I'm not crazy, I'm quirky. There's a difference," Blue argued, having heard Bernadette's comment.

"That difference is so miniscule that it can't be seen with the naked eye," I said with a pointed look at Blue and then Brea, who was all but bouncing on her skates, ready for an adventure.

"Again I ask, do you really want to get married with a broken nose?"

I smiled at her and said, "Bring it."

"No hitting!" Pandora snapped. "Cheese and rice, the two of you are like children!"

"Say it, Pandora. Just once. Come on," Paula teased. "You can do it."

"I will not stoop to your level," Pandora said primly.

"And now she's talking shit on the vertically

challenged people," Paula grumbled. "Fuck all of y'all. I hope when you do get mugged, his knife is bigger than yours."

"I'm packing a gun too. Preacher insisted," Blue said with a nonchalant shrug before she turned to go back to the bench.

"Oh my God, why didn't I stay at the hotel?" Bernadette hissed.

Maylee patted Bernadette on the arm and whispered, "You'll get used to them over time, babe. I promise."

I laughed when Bernadette replied, "That's what scares me."

"Okay, here's the plan," Paula said firmly. "Blue, you're gonna go find one of the Ares guys and hand over your gun. Then we'll catch the subway and see what sorts of wild shit we can find. If all else fails, we'll go to Coney Island, and you can walk down the street clinking bottles together calling for the Warriors to come out and play."

"But if we're gonna do that, don't I *need* the gun?" Blue argued.

"Absolutely fucking not," I snapped, knowing there was no way we'd be in danger with my brothers' men following us all over town. "You will not get into a shootout on the fucking subway!"

"All of you are no fun at all," Blue grumbled.

"Fine. I've got a challenge for you," I said with a wicked grin. "If you can make it all the way around the rink

- *without falling or holding onto the rail* - I'll let you carry your gun on the subway."

"Do I have to do that too?"

"Are you serious right now, Brea?" Paula shrieked.

"Oh my God," Matalie said as she leaned forward against the barrier and rested her head on her folded arms. "Two felons carrying guns they're not even supposed to have, looking for crimes on the street so they can go vigilante on some unsuspecting mugger. It's like a really bad B-movie plot. I can't think of a single defense that would hold up in a court of law, even if I *were* licensed to practice here."

"Yes, Brea, you have to do that too," I said with a pointed look. "Anyone else carrying illegal weapons I should know about?"

Jenn slowly raised her hand, and I heard Blue laugh before she said, "I'm not a felon. Does that count for anything?"

"Nope," I snapped.

"Okay then," Jenn said with a shrug. "My ass is *not* going out there, so I'll give my gun up to one of the guys willingly."

"I'm carrying Enzo's switchblade, and I think that might be illegal."

"Knives don't count, Maylee," Paula assured her. "If they did, my ass would be out there on the ice trying to make it around without embarrassing myself too."

"Lace up, bitch. Looks like we're going skating!"

"I don't know," Brea hedged as she looked from Blue out over the ice. "That thing is really big around, and it's gonna hurt . . ."

"That's what she said!" Paula, Bernadette, Matalie, Jenn, and Maylee said in unison.

"You don't have a single hair on your ass if you don't take the challenge Frankie threw out," Blue said as she tightened her skates again.

"I'd like to think she doesn't have a hair on her ass anyway," Jenn chimed in. "Just saying."

"I don't know . . ."

"I triple dog dare you, Brea," Blue said as she slowly nodded and stared at our friend. "Triple dog."

"What are we, 10?" Brea snapped.

"Chickenshit," Paula teased.

Pandora grinned at Brea. "You're gonna back down from *that?* Really?"

"So we're all 10-year-olds now. Great," Bernadette mumbled.

"Either take the challenge or give up the guns," Maylee reminded them. "It's up to you."

"I can do this!" Brea boasted. "I can. Just watch me!"

"Says the woman who has a standing appointment with her chiropractor because she gets injured during sex," Matalie reminded her.

"Fuck you," Brea muttered as she hobbled toward the entrance with Blue a few feet behind her. "We're doing this. It's the point of the matter now."

"Yeah! We're fucking doing this!" Blue cheered.

The rest of us, our shoes on now, walked back to the barrier to get a front row seat to Blue and Brea's destruction, as good friends should. I called out a reminder, "Stay away from the wall, ladies."

Brea and Blue shot me the bird before they pulled their gloves back on and stepped out onto the ice .

"Once they fall and can't get up, how are we going to get them out of there?" Jenn asked. I glanced over and realized that Maylee, Matalie, Pandora, and Paula all had their phones out to record the chaos. "They should have patrols out there, like lifeguards."

"You got my mom to try?" Sis asked as she stopped near us with August close behind.

"It was a triple dog dare," Paula explained.

"Oh, so she had no choice." Sis nodded slowly and then gasped when Brea started to wobble. "We're gonna have to carry them to the car when they're done."

"We're going to ride the subway and see if we can find some adventure," Matalie explained. "Are you girls in?"

"Do we have to circle around again? Because if we do, I'm out," August said with an exaggerated wince. "I think I broke my tailbone twice already."

"Me too," Sis agreed.

"They're only doing it because they have to give up the guns they're carrying if they can't do a lap without falling," I explained.

"Well, shit," Sis grumbled as her head fell forward and touched her chest.

"I guess I'll go another round," August said with a sigh.

"All of you are fucking certifiable!" Matalie shrieked. "What is wrong with you people?"

"If you don't want to go again, just give your gun to one of the Ares guys to take back to the hotel," I explained.

"That sounds like a better plan," August said as she clutched at the wall and slowly started inching her way toward the opening. "My ass hurts, and I think I pulled a hammy."

"I think I pulled an everything," Sis grumbled as she followed August. "I guess I don't bounce like I used to."

The women around me gasped ,and Paula exclaimed, "Oh! Oh! She's got it. She's . . ."

Maylee laughed. "She definitely doesn't have it."

"Nooo!" I heard Blue scream as Brea fell right into her and they hit the ice in a tangle of limbs.

They managed to get sorted out and then laid in the middle of the rink like starfish as people skated around them.

"Who has to go rescue them?" Maylee asked as Blue rolled over and got to her hands and knees. She crawled over to Brea and stared down into her face, and I couldn't help but laugh at the forlorn expressions they had. "Oh look! Saint and Torpedo have got them!"

"If they can quit laughing long enough to help," Matalie said through her own giggles.

"I guess they're the lucky winners of the take the guns away from the felons game," Maylee said as she leaned against the rail and wiped tears of laughter from her cheeks. "I swear, every day I spend with all of you is an adventure no matter what."

"I'd say we have years of adventure left, but from the looks of Blue and Brea, they might have to sit a few out after tonight," Paula said as we watched Blue start to fall again and almost take Torpedo down with her before he managed to steady them both. "They're gonna be hurting tomorrow."

"Almost as bad as the guys will after their golfing adventure," I mused. "Christopher was asleep in the tub when I left the hotel."

"Boss was on the bathroom floor," Jenn said with a grin.

"Hook was feeling frisky but passed out about three seconds after we laid down"

I laughed at the look of frustration on Paula's face and sighed. "It's going to take everyone a week to recover once the wedding's over."

"If we don't find them a chiropractor, they won't make it a week," Maylee said with a wince as Brea fell again. "Damn. Those women are gonna be hurting tomorrow."

"Look at us," Paula said as she nudged Matalie with her shoulder. "We're the smart ones who didn't risk it going out on the ice."

"I triple dog dare you to go out there in your shoes and do a pirouette like a ballerina," Sis said with a grin.

"Nope!" Paula said as she shook her head. "I'll take all sorts of risks, but ending up in a full body cast is not my cup of tea."

11

BLUE

"It's not the landing that gets ya, it's all the acrobatics you do while you're trying *not* to fall that do you in," Hammer said over his cup of coffee. "If you'd have just let yourself relax, you'd have probably been just fine."

"Jude, if you have any love for me at all, you'll find a balcony and throw him off of it so I can watch *him* bounce," I growled as I glared at Hammer.

"I've been dying to do that for years," Jude grumbled. Then, with a frown, he mimicked, "No fighting, Preacher! Don't hit him, Preacher! Settle down, Preacher!" He sighed and, in his regular voice, said, "It gets monotonous."

"How are you feeling, Blue?" Sis asked as she sat down across from me with her own breakfast plate.

"I fall to pieces . . ." Hammer started singing that old Patsy Cline song, and it was all I could do not to reach across the table and stab him with my fork. When I glared at him, he just grinned and took another bite of his omelet.

"I'm sore. How's your mom?"

"She's okay, I think. She was up and around earlier. Said her elbow hurts but the fall . . ."

". . . and I can't help falling . . ." I heard a growl when Hammer started singing Elvis and then realized it had come

from me when Jude burst out laughing.

Sis managed to stifle her own laugh and asked, "What hurts the most?"

"Is being so close . . ." Hammer started singing, and I couldn't help but stare at him in question. He kept going, and I tried to figure out what the hell *that* song had to do with me falling until Sis helped him with the chorus.

"And having so much to say and watching you walk away . . ." Sis belted out the lyrics to the Rascal Flatts song in perfect harmony with Hammer.

"He's corrupting the children, Boss! I told you not to let him stick around!" Jude snapped.

"Okay, that was reaching," I argued, interrupting Jude's tirade.

"I keep on fallin' . . ." Hammer managed a decent impression of Alicia Keys.

"There ya go," I bitched. "Now I want to kill you again."

"Can we go one single day without me having to separate you two like children?" Boss asked before he closed his eyes and took a sip of his coffee. "There's a monkey on meth playing cymbals inside my skull and aliens trying to claw their way out of my eye sockets right now. If I get into the middle of your shit, everyone in this room is going to end up dead."

"This might help you, sir," Freda, one of the women from the hotel who always seemed to work the breakfast shift, said as she set a bottle of Gatorade next to Boss's elbow. She put another in front of Hammer and slid one across the table to Jude with a smile.

"Thank you, Freda," Jenn said as we smiled at her. "How did you know they might need that?"

"My sister, Shonda, works the front desk. She said the men were in quite a state when they got back yesterday, so I had one of the guys stock up," Freda explained.

"Oh, I met Shonda!" Pandora said from her spot close to the end of the table. "So that means your sisters with Lorena?"

"Who's Lorena?" Kitty asked.

"She's the nice lady who brought food for Jared the other night when we were trying to get him to go to bed," Pandora explained.

"Oh! Sweet lady," Kitty said with a nod before he took a bite of his apple. "She even came all the way back up to bring him chocolate milk a little bit later."

"That reminds me. I need to find Olivia and ask her where she got that lotion she gave us," Matalie said as she twisted around in her chair. "I know this is a huge place, but do you know her, by chance? She brought fresh towels to our room the other day and I asked if there was a drugstore nearby because I forgot my lotion. She brought me a bottle that is just divine."

"She actually makes that herself," Freda explained as she added a selection of Gatorade to the juices in the trough of ice on the sideboard. "I think she works this evening. I'll make sure she comes to talk to you."

"Thanks!" Matalie said with a smile.

"Have a pleasant day," Freda said before she tucked the empty tray under her arm and walked toward the door. "Please ring if there's anything else I can get you."

"The people who work here are so dang nice," Pandora said as she cut up a piece of melon for Jared.

"My guess is that even though we're a pain in the ass, they probably like us better than any of the other guests because we're not uptight assholes," Boss surmised. "When do you think the last time a group of women staying in this hotel started up a conversation with any of the kitchen staff or someone from housekeeping?"

"I would guess that never happens," Frankie said from where she sat at one of the other tables.

"Is your family nice to them, Frankie?" Hadley asked.

"I know they're nice to the people they come into direct contact with, but in their defense, this hotel employs hundreds of people. There's no way they know them all."

Jenn agreed, "Well, everyone we've met so far is really nice. Your family has been so kind to us."

"Hopefully, your brothers aren't as hungover as us. If they are, they'll never forgive us," Stamp said as he propped his arm on the table and rested his head in his hand. "I'm too old for this shit. My whole body hurts."

"How's Matteo?" Paula asked Stamp.

"He's fine. The young ones recover quicker, I guess," Stamp said before he tipped up his Gatorade.

"I think my whole butt is bruised," Harper moaned. "I may have broken something from falling on it so much."

"Where's Brea?" Hannah asked.

"Traction," Paula said with a giggle.

"When I talked to Chef this morning, he said that Brea was floating in the tub and the only thing she'd move was her foot to reach up and add hot water when the water got too cool," Hook said.

"We've all got a few hours to do our own thing this morning. Is everyone staying around here or what?" Jenn asked.

"I'm going to hang out with my friend Carol," Bernadette told us.

"Hook asked me to take him to some places I remember from when I was a kid," Paula explained. "What are you guys going to do?"

"Jude and I are going to go to the 9/11 memorial and then roam around," I explained. "He found a website that has some cool places from history and movies. Anyone want to go with us?" Several of our friends wanted to go with us, and within just a few minutes, we'd made a plan for the day. "Who volunteers to go up and try to talk Brea into coming with us?"

A resounding chorus of "Not it!" sounded from around the room followed by more laughter.

As Jude explained the sights he planned to see, I leaned over and smiled at Frankie. "Thanks for bringing us to New York, friend."

"It's been a great adventure so far, hasn't it?"

"There's been so much *adventure* that I don't think anyone's taken time to ask how you're doing. Are you ready to be married to my brother?"

"More than ready."

"You know that means you and I are going to be sisters, right?"

"That's terrifying," Frankie teased.

"My family's moving up in the ranks because of you," I told her with a smile. "We went from petty criminals, convicts, and murderers to mafia. The only criminal enterprise that's higher than that would be congress or the presidency, and I highly doubt any of us are willing to get that dirty."

"There's always Preacher's family," Frankie suggested with a shrug. "Then you'd be surrounded by crooks, huh?"

"Since we're going to be part of the whole organized crime scene, you've got to tell me some of the secrets, right?"

"Like what?"

"Where is Jimmy Hoffa really buried?"

"Honey, you know Hoffa was from Detroit and not New York, right?"

"But it's really all connected, isn't it?" Jude leaned in to hear Frankie's answer, but I could tell from the look in her eye that she was about to say something that was going to throw him into a tailspin just because she could.

"Okay, I'll tell you this one little secret," Frankie said in a conspiratorial whisper. "Hoffa was put into witness protection by the FBI, and they moved him to New York so the families could keep an eye on him. Since he wasn't allowed to work with the teamsters anymore or tell his stories to the public, he chose a different path."

I glanced at Jude and saw that his eyes were wide, and he was hanging on Frankie's every word. I took a deep breath and waited for it, and she didn't disappoint.

"What they didn't know was that he was a really good artist, and he hooked up with this old friend of his who was a really good businessman. They made a plan, and even though it took them a while to execute it, all that information he wanted to give out was slowly fed to the media."

"What?" Jude whispered.

"Yep," Frankie said with a grin. "His friend started making television shows and put easter eggs in almost all of them, giving people hints about mafia secrets."

"Secrets?"

"Yeah, Preacher. *All* the secrets."

"Like what?"

"They unmasked at least one bad guy in each episode of the series."

"Really? What show?"

"And then they'd get in their van and go off to the next adventure only to find another bad guy who was hiding."

"What show? How have I never heard this?"

"They showed hundreds of them," Frankie insisted. "*Hundreds!*"

"What?"

"I'm serious, Preacher."

I let my chin rest on my chest as I tried my hardest not to crack a smile.

"And there is one definite way to know exactly when they're about to give away a secret."

"How?"

"I can't tell you," Frankie said as she sat up straight again and shook her head. "I just can't."

"Are you fucking serious right now?" Jude snapped. "You can't lead me on like that and then shut down. People have a right to know this shit, Frankie."

"I just don't think I can do it," Frankie insisted sadly.

"I'll pay you," Jude offered.

"No, money means nothing to me when it's something this important."

"Would you do it for a Scooby Snack?" Captain asked Frankie with a deadpan expression.

Without skipping a beat, Frankie did the most flawless impression of Scooby Doo that I'd ever heard and said, "Scooby Dooby Doo!"

The room erupted in laughter, and I couldn't help but join in as Jude scowled at Frankie. Finally, after it started to die down, Jude said, "I hate all of you. I can't believe I fell for that. Total bullshit."

Frankie instantly sobered and leaned toward Jude one more time as she whispered, "But is it?"

PAULA

"I never imagined I'd be walking down these streets again," I said as Hook and I stopped at an intersection to wait for the light to change.

"Well, here you are. How does it feel?"

"Not as good as I'd imagined," I admitted. "I think having you here with me is the best part, though."

"That makes me feel good," Hook said as he squeezed my hand and smiled down at me. The light changed, and we walked across the street with all of the other pedestrians. "So what are we looking at here?"

"We used to stop by this place to buy candy on the way home from my dad's office," I said as we got closer to a small convenience store that had been in the neighborhood since my parents were young.

We stopped in front of it and looked through the window before Hook said, "They're open. Let's go in."

"Oh, I don't know . . ." I hedged. He tried to pull me closer to the door, but I stood my ground.

"What's wrong?"

"I've had it in my head for almost a decade that I can never show my face around here again. Now I'm all over the place with the girls, taking pictures with strangers at the diner and . . . it's just a lot."

"Since when do you shy away from *anything?*" Hook asked.

I took a deep breath and glanced inside the store again. He was right. I wasn't in danger anymore. My father was still alive but he was 'neutralized,' according to my brothers and my son. My son was in charge of the family that had wanted me dead and that gave me a blanket of protection that was better than the guard who'd been discreetly following me and Hook since we left the hotel.

Why the hell couldn't I walk into that store like I'd done for years when I was younger?

"Fuck it. Let's go inside. I want some candy."

"That's my girl," Hook said as he squeezed my hand. He held the door open for me, and as I walked inside, I was assaulted by the same smells I remembered from my childhood. It didn't seem like much had changed since the last time I'd been here, so I guessed the candy I'd been craving for ages was still in the same place.

"Which candy do you want?" Hook asked as he turned left down an aisle. "I think I want some taffy."

"I always got the bags of candy on the back wall," I said as I slowly walked toward the back of the narrow store. I looked left and right, occasionally stopping to peruse the shelves but stopped in my tracks when I heard a man's voice I never imagined I'd hear again.

"I always kept a bowl of these on my desk."

"I remember you bought a bag at least once a week," the sweet woman who owned the shop replied.

My feet had a will of their own, and I found myself standing next to the man in the dark suit. I was just a bit behind his shoulder, so I could see him in profile even though he hadn't noticed me.

"Well, now that I'm retired, I won't be coming around as often, I suppose. Give me three bags."

"When did you retire?" the woman asked with an uncomfortable glance over his shoulder, probably looking for his ever-present guards who seemed to enjoy intimidating people. I turned to make sure none of them were behind me and realized the only guard in the store was there to watch over *me*.

"Well, it's not official yet but . . ."

"But things are changing at a rapid rate, aren't they, Father?" I blurted out and then smiled when he jumped like he'd just been touched by a live wire. He spun around and stared at me in shock, and I heard the woman behind the counter gasp when she recognized me. "It seems those skeletons in the closet aren't just rattling anymore; they're up and moving around the city without anyone to stop them."

"Paola?" the dear woman's voice sounded uncertain.

I smiled at her and reached for a bag of the candy that I'd always loved. Once I'd set it on the counter, I glanced up at my father and asked, "You'll take care of this for me, right? For old times' sake?"

I could see the vein in his temple throbbing and wondered about the mottled red tone his skin had taken. It would bring me so much joy if the man would just stroke out right here in the middle of the store, taking his last breaths on the scuffed linoleum, but I wouldn't be so lucky.

"What are you doing in my town?" my father growled.

I laughed softly, knowing that would enrage him more than anything. Well, almost anything.

"But it's not your town anymore, is it?" I laughed again and grinned at him as I said, "It seems as if the roles have changed. Now I'm welcome here and you're not. Funny how things worked out, isn't it?"

"You *are* Paola," the woman whispered.

"Not anymore," I said as I shook my head. "I'm Paula now."

"Hey, little one, I got you a handful of kisses. Did you find what you were looking for?" Hook asked as he walked up beside me. He looked at my father's angry face and tensed before he asked, "Is everything okay?"

"Everything's just fine," I said as I took the candy out of his hands. I set it on the counter next to my father's selection and my own and said, "We'll go ahead and buy his too. That way he can think of me every time he reaches for his favorite candy."

We were silent as the woman rang up the purchases, and Hook never took his eyes off my father as I passed the woman a twenty-dollar bill.

"Do me a favor, please. Put the change down as credit for my father's next purchase. I'd hate for him to miss out on one of his favorite things now that his situation has changed."

"Paola . . ."

"I'm no longer the girl you can push around, Father," I assured him as I reached for the bag of candy the woman held out to me. "You have no power anymore, and that's gotta sting. But them's the breaks, right? Enjoy your *retirement*."

I took Hook's hand and walked away without so much as a backward glance, my eyes on the guard who was watching my father's every move, ready to duck or run, depending on his reaction. When he did nothing but stare, I walked past him out the door and turned right.

We hadn't gone far when Hook squeezed my hand and asked, "That was your dad, wasn't it?"

"Sure was. Look at me all responsible and shit. I didn't even stab him in the eye like I've been dreaming about doing for more than 20 years."

"We could go back if you want," Hook offered.

I laughed and shook my head. "No. I like how that went. He knows I'm here and walking around free, and there's nothing he can do about it. It's liberating."

"I bet."

"We can come visit whenever we want."

"Now that things have changed, do you want to move back to New York?"

I looked at him in shock and asked, "Would you move here? What about Tonya?"

"I'm asking if that's what you want," Hook pushed.

"Hell no. It's freezing here. If we were at home, I'd be sitting out by the fire pit with the girls drinking wine wearing shorts with bare feet."

"Good."

"You can't get rid of me that easily," I teased.

"I wouldn't know how to live without you. I wouldn't want to try."

"I'm in this for the long haul, sweetheart. Glad to hear that you are too."

We walked in silence for a while longer and then stopped at a crosswalk as we got to a busy intersection. Finally, Hook broke the silence by asking, "Can I have my candy?"

"Oh sure," I said as I handed him the small paper sack.

"Hold this for me," Hook said as he put something in my hand.

The light changed and people swarmed around us, but I was rooted to the spot as I stared at the ring Hook had handed to me. I turned to look at him and realized he wasn't standing next to me anymore. Instead, he was down on one knee staring up at me.

"I love you, little one, and I'm going to keep loving you until I take my last breath. Now it's up to you whether that's by your own hand or you let nature take its course," Hook said with a nervous laugh. "But, either way, my life isn't complete without you. Will you marry me?"

"You want to get married?" I whispered.

"I want to spend the rest of my days watching you smile and making you laugh, whether you take my name or not."

Time seemed to stand still as the frigid wind cooled the hot tears on my cheeks, and Hook stared at me with love in his eyes. I rested my hand on his cheek as I leaned down and kissed him like my life depended on it. And, in a way, it did. My life wouldn't ever be complete without him in it.

"I'd marry you right this second if I could," I whispered before I kissed him again.

He pried my hand open and took the ring out before he slipped it on my finger. Hook kissed the ring and then the back of my hand before he stood, pulling me into his arms and holding me with my feet dangling above the concrete as our mouths met in a fiery kiss.

When we were both breathless, he touched his forehead to mine and said, "For the rest of our lives, New York City will have this memory for us. Every time we visit, we can stop here and remember how we feel right now."

"Really cold?" I joked.

"Yeah, little one. That's what I'm feeling too."

"I love you," I said with a grin as he let me slide down his body until I was back on my feet.

"Let's go back to the hotel, and you can show me just how much."

Hook started walking in the direction we'd come from but stopped when he realized I wasn't beside him. He turned around and asked, "Are you okay?"

"I'm just staring at this rock on my finger wondering if I'm having some sort of hangover hallucination or something," I admitted.

"That is one shiny diamond, isn't it?"

"It is. How long have you had it in your pocket?"

"I've been planning to propose for a while now but wanted to wait until I'd talked to Zach in person before I bought the ring."

"You bought it here?"

"I've found that all the best things come from New York," Hook teased as he wrapped his arm around my waist and pulled me closer. " Stamp's ex gave me one hell of a deal on that diamond."

"You met Marla?" I asked as we started walking again.

"And Carlo."

"That's a blast from the past," I admitted as I looked around the bustling street, wondering how in the world I'd ever missed this now that I'd experienced the laid-back pace of Tenillo. "I don't miss this place at all anymore now that I have a life with you."

"Good because I'm ready to go the fuck home and relax where's it's quiet and calm." Hook thought about what he'd said for a second and then laughed. "Not that life with you will ever be quiet or calm."

"And you wouldn't want it any other way."

12

FRANKIE

"Is everyone ready to get glamorous?" I asked as I walked into the meeting room that the staff had converted to our salon for the day.

"What in the world are we all doing in here?" Blue asked.

"Per the email sent to all of you, this is where we're getting ready for tonight's party," Bernadette barked, still a little bitter that everyone kept asking what was going on or happening next.

"I have some gifts for you," I explained as I motioned toward the couches and chairs that were set up at the end of the room. "The other day when we went to get measured for the wedding attire, I had the staff pay attention to the different dresses each of you commented on and then had the one you seemed to like most delivered for you to wear tonight along with complementary shoes."

"You're kidding," Pandora gasped.

"I know you were all worried about fitting in tonight, and I thought that if we all played dress-up together, you might be a little less nervous." I waved toward one of the staff members, and she opened the doors so that the racks of clothing that had been delivered could be rolled in by a few of the saleswomen who'd been so helpful in the store the other day. "There are a couple for each of you to choose from and shoes to match each. If they need any alterations, there are people waiting to do that too."

"Oh, Frankie," Jenn whispered. "This is too much."

"I know that you put your lives on hold to travel here and stay for a week while you jump through hoops with me. I wanted to thank you by giving you a glamorous fairy tale for at least one night. We still have to go hang out with all the stuffy people, but we'll be together and look fantastic while we do it."

"I was so worried that I didn't have anything fancy enough, and I hated the thought of embarrassing you," Blue admitted. "I was so out of my element when I found out there was going to be a formal event."

"You could show up in a pillow case, and I'd still be proud to tell everyone you are one of my girls," I said honestly. "And I know that the clothes don't make the woman, but they do a lot for her self-esteem, so I thought I'd give everyone a helping hand. Sis and August went with the girls and picked out their dresses this morning. They'll be with us in just a bit."

"This is all so sweet," Pandora said as she hopped up from the couch and rushed toward me. She gave me a tight hug and then pulled away and smiled with tears in her eyes.

"I'm getting my fairy-tale prince, and I wanted to make sure everyone else got their own time to shine too."

"Woman, you're gonna make me cry," Blue said with a sniff as she got up and walked my way. "I want to hate you because I'm about to have to wear a dress and heels, but I can't muster anything up other than happy tears right now."

"As you can see, we've got a hair and makeup team. By the time we leave this room, we're gonna be dolled up like superstars," Bernadette explained. "The guys' suits were delivered, and they'll be getting ready in the rooms while we get ready down here."

"This is so freakin' cool," Brea said as she walked towards me, Blue, and Pandora.

"Paula," I said with mock concern. "Is something going on? You're awfully quiet, and that's not like you at all."

Paula was sitting on the couch by herself almost vibrating with excitement as the women all turned to look at her.

"I'm not sure I'll be able to make it tonight. I mean, it's been kind of hard to walk around all by myself."

"You've always been a tad clumsy, so how does that make today any different than yesterday?" Blue teased.

"Yesterday, I didn't have this fucking boulder on my hand," Paula screeched as she lifted her left hand up and showed off her ring.

The women went wild and swarmed Paula to get a glimpse of the ring. Paula explained that she'd been upset when she first ran into her father, but then she'd felt relieved knowing there wasn't anything he could do to her now. When she told us about Hook's proposal on the corner of a busy street, I saw that more than one of our friends had tears in their eyes just like I did.

"So we have another huge wedding to brace ourselves for, huh?" Blue asked.

"Hell no," Paula scoffed. "When we get a chance, we're going to disappear for a weekend and come back married. I'm not doing *any* of this shit again."

"Thank God," I heard Brea mutter, and I couldn't help but laugh.

"But this week is about Frankie's circus, and we're her monkeys here to dance on command. So let's look at our beautiful gowns and get all dolled up so we can perform tonight."

We laughed at Paula, and I pulled her to my side for a hug. "You deserve the spotlight, too, Picolla. I think I'm going to talk to our brothers and see about getting them to throw a big wedding just like this for you."

"Don't threaten me, Romano, or you *will* walk down the aisle with a broken nose," Paula said with a scowl. She stared deep into my eyes as she yelled, "Blue! Frankie said that she thinks Spencer Reid looks like a mole rat and your dogs are ugly."

"What the fuck did you do that for?" I snapped.

Paula looked down at the engagement ring on her finger and smiled. "I don't want to get blood on my beautiful ring by punching you in the face myself, so I did the next best thing."

"You're a psychopath."

"I know, right?" Paula winked at me and walked

toward the rest of the women.

"Why the fuck are you talking about my dogs, and what did Spence ever do to you, hag?"

Paula laughed and then stoked the fire when she said, "And she asked me if I want to go in halfsies on renting a clown to chase you around on your birthday."

"What the fuck did I ever do to you, Frankie?" Blue yelled as she spun around with a dress in each hand. "That's not even funny."

"Paula's a tiny little psycho. I didn't say any of those things."

"You started it, Frankie," Paula said with an evil laugh. "Don't fuck with the short people, they'll take you out at the knees."

"Isn't that the fucking truth?"

"I feel like a princess," Matalie said as she stepped back from the full-length mirror and turned around to look at the back of her dress. She reached up and touched the earrings that matched the delicate necklace I'd given her and grinned at me in the reflection. "You look stunning, Jenn. Boss isn't going to know what to do with himself."

"There will be no sneaking away to your room until *after* my brothers give their speeches," I warned.

"We're not going to have much choice," Brea argued as she leaned closer to the mirror and studied her painted lips. "When Marques sees me, he's gonna put me over his shoulder and sprint back to the room."

"I've made accommodations that might stop that from happening," Bernadette said from the chair where the woman was putting the finishing touches on her hair. "They're going to meet us in the foyer outside of the ballroom. We're going to get off the elevator about two seconds before we're escorted into the room."

"So it's going to be like a grand reveal?" August asked.

"I'm so excited," Hannah squealed. "Mom, come take a picture of us looking so fancy."

I watched as the girls posed for some selfies with their mom, and then a few of the other girls posed together after one of the ladies who'd done our makeup offered to take a group shot.

"Ladies, just in case I forget to thank you later, I'll say it now. I'm so glad I have all of you in my life, and I can't imagine having anyone else here with me on my big day. I didn't realize what a lonely life Paula and I led until one by one, we met all of you. Now I can't imagine not having umpteen nosy women up in my business, day and night, for the rest of my life."

"You know what, Big City?" Blue started and then grinned when I scowled at her for using the nickname her brother still occasionally used. "Only you could say 'thank you' without really saying it and end with an insult but still make me love you anyway."

"I love you, too, Blue. I know all of you have my back if I need you and would do absolutely anything for me just like I'd do for you.

"You did get some of them into dresses, and I thought there was no way in hell that would ever happen," Maylee admitted. "They must love you very much to even consider it, let alone go through with it. Since you know dressing up doesn't bother me at all, I'll just say that for you, I'd go braless into a grocery store wearing knock-off sandals with rubber heels, a three-day-old messy bun, and a shirt that advertised lawn care products with a stain across the front and a hole in the sleeve."

"Oh my. The horror," Jenn said drolly. "That's what half of us wore on the flight here."

The room erupted into laughter, and I interrupted them with a big smile. "From my heart, ladies. Braless or not, Jimmy Choos or bare feet, Texas or Manhattan, you ladies are part of my heart and soul, and I love you dearly."

"If you make me cry, *I'll* punch you," Jenn said with a sniff. "You know I'm not a crier."

"I can see that," Bernadette said with a sniff. "I'm not either."

"It's time to go downstairs, Ms. Romano," Cassandra, the woman in charge of making sure all of mine and Bernadette's plans had run smoothly while we were here, said from the doorway. "The men have convened in the foyer of the ballroom."

"Let's go wow our men," I suggested.

"You were worried about the men carrying us off to the nearest secluded spot to muss our hair and makeup, but I have a feeling that when I see Boss all dressed up, I'm going to be the one out of control," Jenn admitted. "I make no guarantees that I'll be able to resist."

BOSS

"I swear this fucking thing gets tighter around my neck the longer I stand here," Soda complained from where he was leaning against the wall between Rodeo and Chef. "This is *not* what I signed up for."

"You look good, brother. Sis is gonna shit when she sees you," Captain assured him. "Now stop fucking with it. You're gonna make it crooked."

"Dammit, son," Preacher grumbled. "Let me fix you again." He walked over in front of Soda and adjusted his tie and then smoothed the lapels of his suit before he stepped back. "Stop fidgeting and act like you belong here."

"Fake it till you make it," Santa suggested. "God knows that's what I have to do when Frankie drags me to shit like this."

"Ten years ago, I'd have never imagined I'd be standing in a swanky hotel in Manhattan dressed up in a suit that probably cost more than the house where I grew up, waiting to go into a room packed full of strangers and eat tiny food creations that wouldn't keep an ant alive. It's all your fucking fault, Santa."

Santa looked at Hook like he was nuts. "*My* fault? You're the one that hooked up with Doc. She brought Frankie around in the first place."

"Technically, it's Boss's fault we're here. He took one look at Cool Cat and was lost and then the rest of us fell like dominos. I'm okay with that."

"You're still riding that high from her saying yes instead of stabbing you and disappearing into the crowd, never to be seen again," Kitty teased.

Hook nodded. "I think it was touch and go there for a second. There was a momentary flicker in her eyes, but it went away and she accepted after all."

"If you make us come back here and do this shit again, I'll kill you my damn self," Preacher threatened. "This whole thing is a 'been there, done that' situation that I'm not willing to repeat."

"You're still hungover, huh?" Rodeo asked.

Preacher's face fell, and he looked sad enough to cry. "Fuck yes, I am. I don't know how people do that shit all the time."

"I'm with you. I haven't felt this bad since I ended up on the bottom of a dogpile in the middle of Soldier Field, and I was fucked up for days after that."

"Chef, we don't want to hear about your sexual

exploits before you met Brea," Bug teased.

"I'll fuck you up, firebug," Chef threatened.

"Why the fuck do we have to go to this thing tonight anyway?" Preacher asked.

Stamp replied, "Frankie's brothers are hosting this as sort of an introduction to polite society around here. For years, our families lived on the fringe, loaded rich and running things but still considered outsiders who weren't fit to invite to the more elegant affairs. None of the men who were in charge ever helped the community, they mostly just hurt it with crime like embezzlement and shit. The four families want to make a change, kind of like we did at home, while still running things their way."

"What does that have to do with the fucking wedding?" Kitty asked.

"They'll know exactly who Paula is the second they see her. Same with me. They might have seen me on television but know I was run out of this town because I killed one of the higher-ups without it being sanctioned by my family. Frankie is the princess who refused to have anything to do with her family's business and was *very* vocal about how she didn't appreciate how they were handling things." Stamp paused and laughed with the rest of us because we all knew how vocal Frankie could be when she disagreed with someone. "Anyway, the fact that we're all friends and here together is going to show the rest of the players in this big, fucked-up game that all bets are off since the four families are united. Frankie's brothers will dance with Paula, Paula's son will dance with my Birdie, my sons will be seen making toasts and sharing conversation with Zachary, his uncles, *and* the

Romanos after decades of tense history."

"It's all a show?" Preacher asked.

"Not at all. It's for real, and this is the first public showing of it. Paula's brothers have an announcement to make that's going to send ripples through the state. Hell, all over the fucking country. Up until tonight, everything has been speculation on the street and among the cops, FBI, and the press. When they see this show of force and how the four families are interacting with each other, and for a good cause, no less, it's going to cement how they want the future to play out."

"And all of us getting dressed up and schmoozing with the socialites of this town does what?"

"I'm not sure if it does anything besides give people an idea of what they might be up against if they get their hands on one of our women, namely Paula, Frankie, or Birdie. You've got to admit that we can be an intimidating bunch when we're together wearing our game faces."

"Birdie's in it, too, just by marrying you?"

Stamp shrugged at Rodeo's question. "It's part of the name, and it's not a secret that she's my old lady."

"They could use Santa and Hook against the family now, too, just like they could use you?" Preacher asked.

Hook let out a bitter laugh before he said, "They could try."

"We'll be fine at home," I assured the men. "We've got our own shit to worry about, and we've got enough eyes and ears around now that we'll know if anything starts to get fishy. We take care of our own."

"Damn right," Chef growled.

"Get your fucking hand off that tie, Soda," Preacher snapped. Soda frowned and dropped his hand with a tortured sigh, and I laughed along with the others.

"Here they come," Rodeo said as he pushed away from the wall, watching the lights above the elevator that was reserved for the floors we were using start to count down.

"Thanks for doing this, you guys. I know this wasn't what you were expecting when I asked you to stand with me at my wedding."

"Anytime, Santa. We're here for you, even if we do have to dress like trained monkeys," Bug assured him. "That's what brothers do, right?"

"Hell yeah it is," I agreed as I turned and waited for my woman to get off the elevator. The doors started to open, and I could hear the women chattering before I said, "Here we go."

The ladies all stood still for a second and smiled as their eyes found their men. I could see Jenn standing at the back of the elevator next to Blue and Brea, and I waited patiently for the rest to clear out so I could get a good look at her.

I felt my heart stop before it started again, racing at the sight of the beauty before me as she walked my way.

"You look stunning, my love," I said as Jenn stopped

in front of me.

"You look so handsome," Jenn whispered as she ran her hands over my lapels. She stared up into my eyes, and I saw all the love in her heart for a second before she grinned. "I might want you to dress like this all the time now."

"Not likely," I scoffed. I took her hand and then stepped back so I could study her from head to toe. Her hair was put up in an intricate style and her makeup made her look like a movie star. The dress she was wearing fit her like a second skin and showed me all the delectable curves I'd enjoyed for the last few years and planned to enjoy for the rest of my life. "Goddamn, baby, you look good enough to eat."

"So do you."

"What do you say we sneak away in a little bit and find a secluded corner so I can explore you with my hands instead of just my eyes?"

"I think that sounds like a great plan, but we promised Frankie we'd wait until after the dancing starts."

"Are you wearing anything that's gonna get in my way?" I asked, imagining what might be under that fancy gown.

Jenn stepped closer and discreetly slid her hand down to rub my cock. "I planned for this and wanted to make sure there was *nothing* in the way of what we both want."

"Oh, fuck me," I groaned.

"And while we're inside, schmoozing with all those strangers, I want you to think about what's waiting for you under this gorgeous dress."

"You're an evil, evil woman."

"And?"

"I love you all the more for it, and I'll show you how much more shortly."

"I can't wait."

RODEO

"Do you feel like a bug under a microscope or is that just me?" Hammer asked from his chair beside mine.

"No, that's exactly what I feel like."

"Same," Bug said from across the table. "But can you blame them? It's not like we fit the mold."

"Hell, I've spent plenty of time with Frankie's family and Paula's too. How the hell do they fit in here? I don't get it," I said as I looked at all the posh people mingling while we waited for dinner to be served. I glanced over to make sure August was okay and saw that she was still in the clutches of Frankie's aunts and cousins right along with Sis. "Soda, are you dead, friend?"

"Don't I wish," Soda grumbled. "I feel like if I were on the television in some of these people's houses, they'd try to adjust the color settings."

The table erupted in laughter, and Soda shook his head with an embarrassed smile.

"You know, all these people dripping in diamonds and shit are probably up to their damn ears in debt. I bet their liquid assets don't amount to much more than ours, and if you break down their debt to income ratio, they're just as broke as everyone else."

"Preacher's got a good point. It takes a lot of money to maintain this lifestyle," Captain agreed. "I'd rather drive my 10-year-old truck that's paid off than have all the bells and whistles I'd have if I were trying to keep up with the neighbors."

"Luckily, *we're* your neighbors," I reminded him.

"I'll give you a ten to take the entire tray of those little crispy things from the waiter next time he walks past us," Hammer said as he watched some men standing near us each take a bite-sized hors d'oeuvre and nibble while they talked. "I'm fucking hungry and giving me food one bite at a time just makes me cranky."

"I took one off a tray earlier that looked like a little piece of bread. I bit into the damn thing and it was filled with some sort of smelly cheese and fish," Soda grumbled. With a forlorn look, he sighed and said, "I'd kill for some good barbecue right about now."

"Me too," Chef agreed. "Even better, give me a big ass steak, a baked potato with everything, and a basket of bread."

"Frankie promised we'd get some food tonight. If she was referring to these little bullshit bites of unidentifiable shit, you better go ahead and run before you're roped into this legally," Soda warned Santa.

"And why the fuck can't I just get a bottle of beer? Man, fuck this fancy shit," Boss said with a glare aimed at Santa.

"These are just the appetizers, guys," Santa assured all the cranky men. "We're gonna have dinner in a few minutes, and then we'll do the dancing shit. Frankie's already arranged for pizzas to be delivered after we get back to our rooms."

"Better be some beer with those," Boss snapped.

"I'm sure there will be," Santa replied. "But look at our women, guys. All dolled up and mingling with the fancy folks. I think we're the luckiest men in the room."

"That's the damn truth," Preacher agreed with a grin. "They're fancied up with their hair and faces all done. You know what that means, right?"

"Oh, I know what that means to me," Boss said with a wicked grin.

"It means every damn one of us is gonna have to rub their feet when the night's over," Stamp said knowingly. "We might get some of the good stuff later, but they're all gonna be bitching that their feet hurt while we eat dinner. Just watch."

"Paula's gonna have her shoes off within the hour, I guarantee it," Hook said with a laugh. "I'd bet Blue does the same."

Preacher laughed. "I wouldn't bet against it."

"What are you boys over here laughing about?" Brea asked as she approached the table. Rather than sit in the chair next to Chef, she perched on his leg and draped her arm over his shoulders. He was perfectly content with her there, but she suddenly stood with wide eyes and sat down in the chair beside him and rested her hands in her lap. "Shit. I forgot where we were for a minute."

"I liked where you were sitting before, Pickle. Come back."

"No, Marques. We're among some of the most elite socialites. They're already eyeing us like they're afraid we're gonna steal the silver."

"Fuck them," Chef grumbled. "They can all go to hell."

"We just have to hold out a little longer," Santa assured us.

I watched August and Sis break away and start toward us, and the other women seemed to gravitate toward them, chatting as they walked across the dance floor toward our group of tables.

"What are you grumps over here mumbling about?" August asked as she sat next to me. I reached for her hand and pulled it into my lap as she rested her head on my shoulder.

"The animals at the zoo are restless. Apparently, it's feeding time," Frankie said as she sat down next to Santa. "I could see all of you snapping and snarling from across the room."

"How much longer, Hince?"

Just then, we heard, "Ladies and gentlemen," as Vincente Moretti, Paula's oldest brother, walked across the raised stage holding a microphone. "If you'll take your seats, dinner will be served momentarily. I'd like to thank you for your support tonight and ask for a round of applause for Francesca Romano and her fiancé, Christopher Miller, who so graciously arranged to support this cause as part of their wedding festivities. As many of you know, there have been some changes recently that are reflected in the crowd you see around you. Tonight, as my brother Antonio and I have recently done in our daily business dealings, I'll hand over control to my son, Cento, and my nephew, Tonio, so they can act as your hosts for this evening."

I looked around and saw shock on many faces and heard frantic whispers as people in the room processed what Vincente had just said - that he and his brother had handed over the reins of the family to their sons.

"And so it begins," I heard Paula whisper.

"Thanks, Dad," Cento said as he took the microphone from his father. "As you all know, we're here to celebrate the impending union of Francesca, a dear friend and the saving grace of my aunt and her best friend, Paola Moretti. Tonight's fundraiser will support a foundation that's close to all of our hearts for many reasons, and we'd like to introduce you to the board members and founders of this worthy cause. We'll hear a few words from some of them and then leave you to enjoy your dinner while we watch a video presentation outlining our plans for the Four Families Foundation."

I leaned back as one of the servers set a plate in front of me and then August. I looked around and realized that almost everyone had been served but were ignoring their food in favor of the activity on the stage.

"Thank you, Cento," Tonio said as he took the mic from his brother. "The Four Families Foundation was started by a group of friends who decided to break the cycle of violence against women and children that has been accepted by generation after generation of not only the families of the board members but many of you here this evening. Tonight, you'll witness something that has taken years to bring to fruition but will last for many generations to come. Let me introduce our good friends, Zach Campana, Matteo and Luca Russo, along with Rico, Ziggy, and Relio Romano."

There was an audible gasp as people around the room realized what this meant, and I couldn't help but smile as I watched Frankie and Paula try unsuccessfully to hold back their happy tears as Stamp grinned proudly at the men on stage.

I looked back to the front of the room and saw the men I'd come to consider friends standing shoulder to shoulder as they looked out over the crowd that included some of the biggest movers and shakers in New York City.

The servers had vanished, and the only people moving in the room now were the photographers and videographers who'd been hired to document tonight's gala.

Paula's son took the microphone from Tonio and smiled at the crowd before he said, "Congratulations, Aunt Frankie. This celebration is all about you and the happiness you've found. I'd also like to take a moment to officially thank you for helping my mom when no one else could. Working together with my friends and associates, we'll try to make sure other women won't be stuck in situations like she lived through. Children won't have to feel powerless like I did while I watched her husband abuse her and her own parents abandon her when she needed them the most."

I saw movement out of the corner of my eye and turned to see Paula take Frankie's hand across the table.

There wasn't a dry eye among us, at least among the women, and I was having trouble breathing past the lump in my throat.

"The Four Families Foundation would like to thank you for joining us tonight, and we ask that you enjoy your dinner while watching the video presentation explaining how we plan to work together to make sure things change for the better, starting today," Ziggy said after he took the mic from Zach. "I hope you're looking forward to dancing after dinner, and don't forget that throughout the evening, winners of the silent auction will be notified personally by one of the Four Families representatives. Thank you."

There was applause as the men filed off the stage and then sat with a few other members of their exclusive group that would now be ruling the New York mafia scene in a way that no one had ever imagined. United. Together.

BERNADETTE

"Damn, woman, I can't wait to get you back to our room so I can peel that dress off of you," Valentine said as pulled me so close, we were touching from chest to knees. "How soon can we leave?"

"We should stay for a while longer," I suggested, even though the idea of rushing up to our room sounded like the best idea I'd ever heard. "Have you danced with Paula and Frankie yet?"

"Yes, Mistress of Ceremonies, I've danced with both of them. We did our part while you were dancing with Paula's nephew and Frankie's brother."

"I should have made a spreadsheet like Blue suggested," I mumbled, wondering if there'd been photo opportunities to get each of them dancing with one from each of the other families.

"You've really embraced this event planning, haven't you?"

"I've enjoyed the hell out of it," I admitted.

Valentine spun me and then maneuvered around Rodeo and August who were dancing almost as close as we were before he said, "I guess that's good since you're gonna be opening a multi-location business that's a partial front for some nefarious mafia shit, huh?" I felt my eyes widen as Valentine grinned. "Are you shocked that I already know, or did you not realize that's what you'd be doing?"

"I'm shocked you already know, but I'd rather believe I'm opening a branch here so Matteo's crush has a place to work."

"Hmm," Valentine said as he looked into my eyes. "If you're not comfortable with . . ."

"If I don't want to do something, then I won't do it. Period."

"That's my girl."

The song came to an end, and I took Valentine's hand and let him lead me back to our table. No one was there, so I looked around the room to find everyone.

"Did they already go upstairs?" I asked in outrage.

"No," Valentine assured me. "They would have taken their suit coats, and isn't that August's shawl?"

"Where the hell are they then?"

"What's wrong?" Frankie asked as she walked up on the opposite side of the table.

"Where did everyone go?" Frankie pointed behind us, and Valentine and I turned just in time to see August and Rodeo walk through the same door all of the servers had been going in and out of all night. "What the hell?"

"It took longer than I imagined it would, but I think they found somewhere they could be a little more comfortable," Frankie said with a grin.

As we watched, Captain and Matalie came back through the doors and stopped at the edge of the dance floor where he spun her before he pulled her into his arms. He said something that amused her, and Matalie threw her head back and laughed. Captain took that opportunity to lean forward and nibble on her neck, and Matalie's laugh stopped as her eyes closed and a look of longing came over her face.

"Fuck this," Valentine said as he started walking, pulling me along behind him. "I bet they've got real food in there. I'm fucking starving."

Once we got across the ballroom, Valentine pushed through the door into the brightly-lit prep area of the industrial kitchen, and we found all of our friends, relaxed and happier than I'd seen them all evening.

"It's about time you got here, brother," Boss said as he lifted his bottle of beer and tipped it toward us. Jenn was perched on Boss's lap and raised one hand in greeting as she lifted a burger to her mouth with the other. "The beer is cold, and the company is a lot better than it is out there."

Chef agreed with a nod before he took a bite of his own burger. "They were hiding the actual food back here this whole time."

Brea breezed over to the table with a beer in each hand and set one down in front of Chef and the other in front of Boss. "They're taking orders right now. You better get back there and talk to Iris if you want something."

"Iris?" I asked.

"She's the really nice lady who found that creamer I wanted," Blue said as she sat down on the other side of Brea.

I heard laughter from the other room and decided to investigate. When I walked through the doorway, I found August perched on Rodeo's lap, and Sis sitting on Soda's. They were sitting at a table with several servers that I recognized from earlier in the evening, and they all had cards in their hands. Preacher was at another table with Bug, Kitty, Captain, and a few more members of the kitchen staff, and they also had a game going, although this one seemed much more serious.

I walked even farther into the room and saw a door with a small window. Through that, I could see Paula and Pandora perched on a counter across from the one where Maylee was sitting, and they were chatting with some women that were assembling burgers. I pushed through the door and Matalie cheered, "Welcome to the party, friend!"

"Is this where all the cool kids hang out?"

"Most definitely," Paula said as one of the women handed her a basket of fries. "Unlimited french fries. Yum."

"They've got *the best* seasoning," Maylee agreed as she picked a fry from the basket beside her. "She said that she'd share her secret if we could guess one of the ingredients."

"How long have all of you been back here?"

"We go back out for a spin around the dance floor with one of the guys and then sneak back in here to hang out. We're still making our appearance, but a person can only take so much," Pandora explained. "Whose turn is it, anyway?"

Paula let out a dramatic sigh. "It's mine. The guys played rock-paper-scissors and Preacher lost. That's cool because Hook danced with Maylee earlier."

"I'm up after you," Pandora said. "I think I've got Soda, but he was grumbling about it, so he may have traded."

I leaned against the counter next to Maylee and sighed. "I wish I'd known all of you were back here sooner. My face hurts from having that stupid fake smile pasted on forever."

"I don't know how you held it together for so long," Paula said with an exaggerated shudder. "I had almost forgotten what it was like to be a Moretti, but it all came crashing back tonight, that's for damn sure."

"They're all watching me like . . . like I don't know

what."

"Back when you lived here and saw someone from one of our families, how did *you* look at them?" Paula asked. I bit my lip, wondering how to best explain it without offending anyone. Paula laughed and then urged, "Come on, Bernadette. Don't be a pussy. Spit it out."

"I always tried to see the difference in us because I thought all of you were criminals and murderers who should be in prison."

"Well, you are quite possibly right about most of them, but then again, look at who you run with now," Maylee pointed out with a bark of laughter.

"True," I agreed. I snagged a french fry and heard Paula growl. After I'd finished it, I reached for another and said, "Those *are* good."

"Delicious," Paula said before she took another bite. "Paprika?"

The woman standing at the grill nodded, and Paula and Maylee let out a whoop of delight.

The door opened, and Boss stuck his head in before he said, "Paula, we're up."

"Shit," Paula hissed as she hopped off the counter and thrust her fries at me. "It's my turn to dance. I'll be back in five minutes."

"I'm next," Pandora said before she took a big bite of her burger. "Are you still hungry, Bernadette? These burgers are delicious."

The woman at the grill looked at me with her eyebrows raised, and I smiled at her before I said, "I'd love a burger if it's not too much trouble."

"No trouble at all," she said as she reached into an industrial-sized refrigerator and brought out a couple of patties. "Double with bacon and cheese?"

My stomach rumbled loudly, and I nodded. "Can you make two of those? I bet Valentine would love one."

"Are you not enjoying yourselves either?" I asked Pandora and Maylee.

"It's not my kind of crowd," Pandora confessed. "I don't know anyone, and when I smile or try to engage any of them in conversation, all they want to do is ask me questions about you, Frankie, and Paula."

"I'm perfectly comfortable out there, but I was having that same issue," Maylee admitted.

"What kind of questions did they ask?"

Pandora looked thoughtful for a second as she finished chewing, then said, "If we're all involved in the family business. Or, this one killed me, if the cowboys in Texas were okay with 'people like us' making our home there."

I snorted with laughter. "They're just all over, huh? Cowboys wearing spurs, tying up their horses in front of the general store."

"I guess," Pandora said as she rolled her eyes. "Marler dragged me back here after he heard me tell a woman that I needed to get back home so I could check my cattle."

Just then, Paula breezed into the kitchen and hopped back up onto the counter so she could dive back into her fries. Before she took a bite, she said, "You're up, chica."

Pandora nodded before she took an enormous bite and delicately wiped her mouth with the linen napkin beside her. She got to her feet and waved at us as she walked out of the room.

"I'm so ready to go home," Paula said softly as she blew out a breath and stared at the floor. Suddenly, she laughed. "I'd have never imagined that I'd be back in New York dying to get back to Texas because I missed my tiger."

"Until you said the tiger part, that sounded pretty normal," I told her with a grin.

"Tiger?" Iris asked as she walked toward me with a plate in each hand. The burgers looked delicious, and I could see steam coming off the french fries that were piled high on the plate. "A *real* tiger?"

I took the plates from Iris before I said, "She's got a tiger, and Jenn has a pet skunk as well as a rooster that comes up higher than my knee."

Iris raised her eyebrows and looked over at Paula. In her thick Brooklyn accent, she asked, "Is this normal?"

"Honey," Paula said as she waved a french fry toward the doorway. "Nothing about any of us is normal, and our pets have nothing to do with it."

14

PAULA

"Now that you're in charge, you won't be able to come to Texas nearly as often," I said as I opened the oven to check on the cinnamon rolls I'd put together for breakfast.

"But you can come see me anytime now," Zach argued. "Me and the guys were joking the other day that whenever we want a dose of reality, we just have to go to Texas."

"What do you mean?"

"Preacher refuses to call me by my name, no matter what I'm in charge of," Zach said with a laugh. "Going to visit you in Texas and hanging out with the guys is humbling, that's for sure."

"If you'd get a decent haircut and quit wearing your hair like that, Preacher and the guys wouldn't give you so much shit."

"Yes, they would! They'd just find something else to give me shit about," Zach argued. "But it's honestly kind of nice."

"I'd imagine it would be hard to get used to your mom asking you to grab some milk when you've got everyone at your beck and call."

"I don't have *everyone* at my beck and call."

"You live in a hotel like that show you used to watch when you were a kid. Oh my God, Zach! You're living *The Suite Life!*"

"I can have you killed. You know that, right?"

"If you don't fall in love with someone named Cody, the universe will weep."

"Mom . . ."

"Zach and Cody. That would almost make up for the 396 million times I had to watch that freaking television show."

"You really don't give a shit about who I am now, do you?"

"Buddy boy, I remember the day you were born. I wiped your ass for years. Even if you were living in the White House, I'd still give you shit."

"I think you would. No fear whatsoever. Poor Hook."

"Boy, I grew up in a house with your grandfather. Nothing you've got going on scares me."

"How'd it feel running into him the other day?" Zach asked.

I leaned forward onto the counter in front of his stool and sighed. "It was sad but exhilarating. Sad that he's my father and there was still a little part of me that wanted him to love me, but exciting because I could look him in the face knowing there wasn't a damn thing he could do to me."

"Not one damn thing," Zach agreed with a nod.

"He looked . . . broken."

"Good. Fuck him." Zach shrugged. "He helped make your life a living hell. I was at the meeting when Uncle Vincente and Uncle Antonio told him he was finished and stripped him of everything. If I'd have been thinking, I'd have taken a video of it just so you could've seen the look on his face."

"I bet it was priceless."

"I thought he was gonna have a fucking stroke. I had sympathy for him until he ordered his guards to shoot . . ."

"He didn't!"

"Oh, he did. But then when his guards just stood there waiting for Antonio and Vincente to tell them what to do, his face just fell. He realized there was no one left in his corner."

"I noticed he didn't have a single guard at the candy store."

"Not one. There were a few holdouts, but they don't work for us anymore."

I burst out laughing, and Zach smiled. "Is that what we're going with?"

"Their employment was terminated."

It broke my heart to think my little boy was cracking jokes about having people killed, but then again, I knew that in the life he'd chosen. it was either him or them. My vote would always be in my son's favor. The rest of them could rot in hell, as far as I was concerned, including my own father.

"And you're being careful?"

"Of course, Mom. I was born for this. I watched how my uncles did things and learned so much from my grandfathers. Watching those two old bastards taught me a lot, especially how they think."

"Like what?"

"They didn't have a single person they could rely on because they treated everyone like shit. There was no loyalty. If they had treated people better, they'd have been loyal, and it wouldn't have been so easy for me or the guys to take over."

"You've learned from their mistakes."

"Damn right."

"I worry because it's just you in charge of the family now."

"No, it's not. Simmy, Cam, and Shy are in it with me. We've all got our strengths, and we play to them as we work together."

"God, it's crazy to imagine your cousins all grown up. Hell, it's crazy that *you* are all grown up."

"Next thing you know, you'll be a grandma."

I stood up and stared at him in shock. "Is there . . . You've got . . ."

"Whoa, hold up. I'm not sure if you're gonna have a stroke or start swinging," Zach said as he put his hands up as if I were trying to rob him. "I don't mean soon. Maybe in 10 or 15 years."

"You're being careful then? And not just with family stuff."

"I wrap my shit up like a Christmas gift every time."

I suppressed a shudder at the thought of my baby boy having sex but nodded. "Good. Keep it up."

"Oh, I don't have a problem with that," Zach teased.

I gagged and shook my head as I closed my eyes and took a few deep breaths. "Puppies, kittens, unicorns, happy clouds with happy trees, chocolate . . ."

"What the hell?"

"I'm trying to think happy thoughts to erase what you just said out of my brain," I snapped as I opened my eyes and glared at him. "Asshole."

"But I'm your favorite asshole, right?" Zach asked, just as the oven timer buzzed.

"Not after that."

"Come on, Mom. You know you love me."

"I'm going to cut you out of the will."

"Do you even have a will?"

"Of course I do."

"You don't need one anymore, Mom," Zach reassured me, "It's going to be okay now. I'll make sure of it."

"That terrifies me even more than living under your grandfather's rule," I admitted. "You promise you'll be careful and make sure and get help from your uncles if you need it."

"Of course I will. I've got the Russo and Romano families to lean on now too."

"You're right, but I'll still worry."

"Isn't that your job?"

"It is, and you're not making it any easier, Twat Knot."

"Hey!"

"Get some plates and forks, please, and refill my coffee while I ice these."

"Yes, ma'am," Zach said as he stood up and started around the bar. "Dammit. You're not supposed to boss me around anymore."

"Whatever. I'm your mother."

"But . . ."

"Boy, do what I said before I thump you."

"No respect at all. None," Zach muttered as he opened the cabinet door.

"Call your friends and see if they're hungry. I have another pan ready to go in the oven, so there'll be plenty."

"Just like old times, huh?"

"No matter how big you are in this town, I'll always be your mom and love you unconditionally, Zach."

"I know. I love you too."

"Good. Now wash your hands and get some napkins."

"Good grief."

"Use soap!"

"No respect," Zach grumbled with a tortured sigh.

When I heard the water come on, I looked over and saw that he was smiling. My little boy may be all grown up now, but he still knew who was in charge. I couldn't help but smile right along with him.

STAMP

"Where's Bernadette?" Matteo asked before he nodded at the doorman and then walked ahead of me out onto the street. "Did she not want to come with us?"

"She went to hang out with her friend Carol again this morning," I explained.

"Carol is the wife that was in the hospital?" Luca clarified.

I nodded and answered, "Yes, that's her. She's been Birdie's best friend since college, I believe."

"And she's doing better now?"

Luca nodded and said, "I was wondering the same thing."

"He hurt her really badly, but she's on the mend, as far as I know. Birdie talks to her pretty often, and she was excited to go see her today."

"She's in limbo," Matteo said before he sighed. "Until we do our thing, she's gonna be looking over her shoulder."

"True. That sucks, man," Luca said. "I wonder if we can move up the timeline. I'll talk to the guys and see what they have to say."

"I'm sure Birdie would appreciate that."

We made small talk as we walked, and when they turned down 77th Street, I knew exactly where they were taking me.

"Oh damn," I said as I caught sight of the bakery at the end of the block. "If you try to walk me past that, I'm gonna disappear inside. You two can go on, and I'll roll my way back to the hotel after I've eaten my fill."

"I remember one of the first times we met you in the city, you mentioned you were dying to have a bagel with cream cheese and lox from this place," Luca recalled.

"Your grandfather used to bring me here when I was a kid," I mused as we stopped in front of the shop that held a million memories of my father and his associates meeting for a quick bite and coffee.

"Well, go in," Matteo said as he held the door open. "Some associates of ours are in town for the wedding, and one of their relatives owns this bakery."

Once I was inside, Luca walked past me and down a short hall where there was a guard standing beside an unmarked door. He opened the door as we approached and then pulled it shut behind us.

"Welcome, my friends," a well-dressed man said as he stood and dropped his napkin next to his plate. He walked around the table and greeted my sons with handshakes before he even glanced my way.

"Moshe Holofcener, this is our father, Valentine Russo."

After Luca introduced me, I stuck my hand out and shook his. "It's a pleasure to meet you."

"And you," Moshe said as he let go of my hand. "I'm glad you could join us for breakfast. Our other associates should be here momentarily. Your son said you had a craving for a good bagel."

"I've been all over the country and eaten in hundreds of different places, but I've never found a bagel with lox that's as good as the ones here."

"Let me introduce you to my friends. Jonah, Zeppo, this is Valentine Russo, Luca and Matteo's father."

I greeted the men with handshakes, and we exchanged pleasantries. We had all just settled down at the table when the door opened again. Luca and Matteo introduced me to their Irish friends, Darragh, Ciaran, and Declan O'Sheeran.

"You look a little shell-shocked, Dad," Luca said as everyone began making their choices from the array of food that had been set out against one wall, talking and laughing as if this were just any normal day.

"I was just thinking that your grandfather is probably spinning in his grave at the thought of you sitting in a room with these guys, just hanging out peacefully. All we need now is . . ." The door opened and Cento Moretti walked in with Ziggy Romano. "Damn. Twenty years ago, I would have *never* imagined any of this shit."

"It's a whole new world," Luca said with a grin.

"A world that all of you are running. It's a pretty monumental achievement, son. I just want you and your brother to be careful, okay?"

"We've got this, man. Don't worry," Matteo said from my other side.

"I understand you left Uncle Don alive."

Luca shook his head sadly and said, "He's been nothing but trouble."

"I've never had any love for Uncle Don. Why didn't you just kill him to send a message?" I asked. I shook my head and sighed. "Fuck. I can't believe I just said that to my kids."

"It's the life, Dad. No sense in trying to deny that," Luca chided.

"We didn't kill him because making him live a miserable life with no power sounded like a more fitting punishment. That's what Vicente and his brother did to their father, and we agreed that it sends a definite message to not only the men who work for us, but our other associates too."

"He's a problem that isn't going to go away quietly," I assured them. "He's been in power since my father died after taking what would have been my place when I went to prison."

"Yes. And now it's our place," Matteo said with an edge to his voice.

"We stripped him of everything. His money, cars, home, and the men who were loyal to him all those years," Luca explained.

"And now he's a desperate man who's as crazy as a shithouse rat and always has been. I know I'm not part of this business, but if I were, I'd vote to put him down like a rabid animal and make *that* a lesson for those who aren't sure of your power."

"If he fucks up even the slightest bit, that's what we'll do. As it stands, he rarely ever leaves his apartment."

"Apartment? He lived in a fucking mansion when my father was killed."

"He currently lives in a one-bedroom walk-up in Longwood," Matteo told me with a grin. "From what I hear, his car was stripped right outside the building a week after he moved in."

"Oh shit," I sputtered out through my laughter.

"Luca and I sat on the hood of his Bentley in front of

his house while our crew packed his shit to be donated to a shelter. We left him with the clothes on his back and two hundred dollars in his wallet. His bank accounts were emptied, his holdings were transferred to our names, and every single thing of worth in his house was donated to a good cause."

"What cause was that?"

"One of the women's shelters where Cento Moretti's mom volunteers," Luca explained. "They had an auction and raised a staggering amount to go toward buying a larger building and hiring more employees."

Matteo chuckled before he said, "Shy Campana is good with computer shit, and he set up an online auction and called it Don's Closet. It was fucking hilarious."

"We took Don's phone and gave him a burner, and every now and then, I'd send him an updated link to the auction site so he could see the progress."

"You boys need to make sure your own safety is covered. Fucking around with him is one thing, but he's a crazy son of a bitch. It would be good that you don't forget that while you're having fun."

"We know. That's why we've got security on all of you, especially the ladies. He's going to do something stupid someday and we'll put him down, but until then, we want him to wallow in his own misery."

"Just be careful. I know you've got the three other families to watch your back, but I still worry. There was a rumor back in the day that Don helped Sal Moretti kill your grandfather. I went to prison, so I never knew for sure, but

I've always wondered." Luca's expression went from laughing and smiling to dark and dangerous in a split second, and when I glanced at Matteo, I saw his had done the same. "He's a dangerous man. So's Old Man Moretti. Don't count either of them out of the game. I'd almost guarantee that both of them have something in the works to come back with guns blazing."

"We'll take your advice to heart," Luca assured me.

"The Four Families are unstoppable now, especially with the help of our friends. Between all of us, we've got the whole Eastern Seaboard covered and on into the Midwest. Hell, we're even working some things out on the West Coast. The world is our oyster."

"Don't forget about Vegas," Luca reminded his twin.

"I'd like to give you some words of wisdom, but all I can really say is don't end up in prison. It sucks there."

Luca and Matteo started chuckling and the O'Sheerans and Moshe, who were sitting across the table from us, joined in.

"We've got systems in place to prevent that," Declan O'Sheeran said with a grin.

"Good. I don't want to have to plan a prison break," I joked. "That's not impossible, considering the firepower in this room, but I'd rather not."

"We'll take care of each other . . . Irish, Jewish, Italian, and even those Texans who are part of our family now."

"That's good to know."

Moshe lifted his coffee mug and said, "Let's enjoy our breakfast, gentlemen. To family."

Everyone around the table lifted their drinks and, in unison, we repeated, "To family."

I felt a little better when I saw one of the Romanos nudge a Moretti with his shoulder before they laughed and said something to Luca. I hadn't been around to watch my sons grow up and was terrified of losing them now, but I knew they were surrounded by some good men.

Unfortunately, it didn't take away any of the fear.

FRANKIE

"Aunt Frankie, look what I made," Freddy, my 11-year-old nephew, said as he skidded to a halt next to my chair. "It's a cyborg hand. I can do anything with it."

"That's cool, bud. You made that?" Christopher asked.

"I did. Olivia gave me the kit for my birthday."

"Olivia? That's your cousin's kid, right?"

I nodded and told Christopher, "She's Guila's daughter. They're the same age."

"I'm never gonna be able to keep everyone straight, I swear," Christopher grumbled before he took another bite of the omelet my brother had made.

"Why don't you try eating with that thing?" my brother, Federico, suggested to Freddy. "You haven't eaten a bite this morning."

Freddy leaned his head back and let out a long sigh of frustration. "Can I eat in the den while I watch TV with the guys? I know you'll probably want to talk about wedding stuff, and I'm over all that."

My brother studied his son for a minute and shook his head. "The world is not ready for a kid like you, I swear."

Freddy grinned and picked up his plate with his free hand and then rushed toward the den where I could hear the television that seemed to stay on day and night.

"He's grown so much since my last visit. It's crazy."

Constance, my niece that I'd nicknamed Stan years ago, laughed from her perch at the bar where she was scrolling through her phone. "I was gone for a week, and when I came back, he was at least six inches taller."

"When I got here earlier, he chewed me out because he'd had to stand still for the tailor *forever* when they had to make last-minute alterations to his tuxedo. Somehow that's my fault."

Stan laughed, "Of course it's your fault. You're the one who's making him get dressed up and stand in front of a million people."

"He's the only kid in either family who's big enough to be in the wedding," Christopher explained.

I nodded. "I would have loved to have Boo and Jared in the ceremony, but they're just too young."

"Well, Olivia's stoked about getting to dress up and be the flower girl," Stan assured me. "As a matter of fact, I need to get going so I can meet her and Guila at the salon. We're getting manis and pedis together and then having lunch afterward before we pick up Olivia's dress."

Stan walked over and gave my brother a kiss on the cheek and then waved at me and Christopher as she called out a goodbye to her little brother and then disappeared down the hall.

"She seems to be handling things well," I pointed out before I took a sip of my coffee.

"She was pretty resistant to the 24-hour bodyguard thing, but she knew it was inevitable," my brother said sadly. "We chose some that were young enough that they wouldn't stand out while they escorted her, and that helped. I had two of my guys on her at first, and she said she felt like she was being followed around by Father Time and his evil twin."

"What about when she's in class?" I asked.

"They're getting a free education out of the deal," my brother told me with a grin. "They're not enjoying that part of the job at all."

"They go to class with her?" Christopher asked with a bark of laughter. "That's funny."

"It's costing me through the nose, but I wanted to make sure they had eyes on her every second."

"Fred," I said, calling my brother by the nickname I'd given him years ago. "You're going to have to let her breathe, or she'll rebel. You know that, right?"

"Sully and Park are good kids. They were raised in the life and understand the importance of her security, but they're young enough that they've become her friends too."

"Friends, huh? And how old are they?" I asked. "What do they look like?"

"Yes, friends, Frank. I was very careful when I selected her guards." I couldn't help but laugh, and my brother glared at me. "If you must know, they're dating each other, *not* my daughter."

"That's awesome," I said as I laughed. "Oh shit."

"Why is that so funny?" Christopher asked.

"Because until a few years ago, that would have been unheard of in our circles. I'm not dense enough to believe that there weren't any gay men in our business, but because of the old school way of thinking, they weren't able to be themselves. I think that's bullshit, and so does the rest of the family."

"Our dad, though, oh no," I said as I shook my head. "He'd have lost his fucking mind. It's a whole new world now that the next generation has taken over."

"Do you need us to do anything before tonight's dinner?" a drop-dead gorgeous man asked from the doorway that led to the hall. I could see another handsome man behind him and was shocked at my sudden realization.

"Those are Stan's guards?" I asked quietly.

"Yep. Both ex-military and their fathers were foot soldiers in Dad's army of minions."

"Good grief," I said as I fanned my face dramatically. "Stan's got some eye candy following her around."

My brother glared at me, and Christopher laughed. "The perfect guards. She can look, but they won't touch."

"Exactly. And since she insisted on getting a place of her own, I made sure there was enough room for them to move in too."

"She's gonna rebel, Fred. Mark my words," I warned.

"Nothing to rebel against," my brother argued with a shrug. "She's got two besties living with her. Beats her arguing with me all the fucking time about her guards."

"My guards never looked like that," I complained. "They weren't very old, but they weren't exactly attractive."

"I know. We started with them, and she complained." I could tell Fred was about to say something that was going to piss me off when he grinned wickedly. "And she called them both Father Time. How does that make you feel?"

"Oh fuck off," I grumbled, and Christopher laughed. "This is my wedding week. You're not supposed to upset me."

"You're right. I'm sorry," Fred said. I thought he was sincere until he smiled at Christopher and said, "I better watch out. If I piss her off, she'll spend even more money."

"The more you talk, the more I feel the need to go shopping on your dime. I think the shoes me and the girls picked to go with our dresses might not work. We may need to go buy more."

"I love you. You're beautiful. You're always right, and you don't look a day over 30."

When I smiled and relaxed in my chair, Christopher ruined it and said, "Shit. I didn't realize it was that easy to tame the beast." I slowly turned my head and glared at him, and Christopher winced.

"Oops. There she is again," my brother said through his laughter. "She's all yours, Santa. Enjoy it."

Christopher leaned over and gave me a quick peck on the lips before he gave me that soft smile that never failed to make me melt. "I can't wait."

15

SANTA

"The ushers can have a seat down in front," Bernadette ordered Zach, Matteo, Luca, and a few other guys whose names I couldn't remember. "I need the groom and his attendants to come up and take their places. Freddy, will you and Olivia tell the ladies that we're just about ready for them, please?"

Frankie's nephew and cousin raced each other down the aisle and laughed when they almost bowled over Soda who was making his way down the aisle toward where Sis was sitting with Frankie's niece, Constance, and her two guards along with Hammer, Rodeo and August.

"Hammer, will you stand where the minister will be?" Bernadette asked as she waved Hammer toward the front.

"Do I get a mic?" Hammer asked.

"No!" Boss, Preacher, and Captain yelled in unison causing everyone in the room to snicker.

"I'm just saying that we should check the sound system while we're here," Hammer said defensively. "Jesus, you guys act like I'm gonna start singing or something."

I walked up the steps to where Bernadette pointed for me to stand and said, "The world is not ready for you to be in stereo, brother."

"Should be. I've got a pleasant singing voice. It's a shame that no one appreciates me."

"I appreciate it when your mouth is shut," Preacher said as Bernadette moved him up a step, making sure the men were staggered down the stairs that led up to the dais where the officiant would stand with me and Frankie.

"Okay. I've got you in the order that the women will come in. There will be a list in the side room to remind you where you're supposed to be in line. It's important that you stay in this order so that we make our exit as couples. That's how Frankie wants it for pictures."

"Got it," Hook said from beside me. "We walk in, stand here and look good until it's all over, then grab our woman and go."

"Not quite, but you're on the right track," Bernadette said with a sigh as she handed her assistant a roll of tape and a pair of scissors. "If you'll mark their spots, I'll go find the women so we can do a run-through."

"There's a whole lot of fucking chairs out there, man," Kitty said from a few steps down. "How many people are supposed to be at this damn thing?"

"Couple hundred, give or take."

"We have RSVPs for 412, so there are enough seats for 550 to be safe," the woman who was marking our spots with tape corrected me.

"Holy shit," I heard one of the guys mutter.

"If *any* of you decide to walk down the aisle and pull some bullshit like this, I will bury you in a field somewhere," Preacher threatened. "This is . . . Oh God. 500 people?"

"You okay, brother?" I heard Boss ask. "You got stage fright or what?"

"Do you even *know* 500 people?" Chef asked.

Hook laughed. "Does Frankie?"

"Man, I got nothing. The only people in this room that matter are the ones on the stage, Frankie, Paula and Stamp's family, and a select few others that I've met in the last few days," I admitted. "The rest are a bunch of people the three of them knew when they lived here and then a shit ton of other people they don't fucking care about."

"Hallelujah," Stamp agreed with a laugh. "Couldn't give two shits about 90% of them."

"This is so fucking crazy," Preacher admitted. "When Blue and I get married . . ."

"According to my sister, that's never gonna happen," I reminded him.

"*When Blue and I get married,* you'd be lucky to get an invite. It'll just be me, her, and the preacher. That's it. Maybe one witness. You guys can duke it out to figure out which one of you it'll be."

"Not it!" I snapped.

"Fuck you, too, then," Preacher said with disgust in his voice. "You're her fucking brother, man."

"Look, it's not that I don't want to come to your wedding. It's just that I don't want to clean up the bloodbath after you untie her and take the gag out of her mouth. That's what it's gonna take to get her in front of a real preacher."

Even Preacher couldn't help but laugh at that image. He nodded as he admitted, "Okay, you might have a point there."

"Me and Paula have already decided that we're gonna elope in Vegas."

I looked out over the seats that were set up in sections, kind of like pews in a church. There was a wide aisle down the middle, and each half of the room was split in half again. All of the chairs had white covers over them with different colors of some see through fabric. I knew from the pictures I'd seen them looking through that there'd be flowers here and there that matched the ladies' dresses.

Honestly, I didn't care what the chairs looked like or what the fuck a jewel tone was. I wanted to have my woman standing in front of me as the preacher tells us to kiss, and then I wanted to take her home where I didn't have to worry about her safety and tuck her away in our house for the rest of our lives.

As far as I was concerned, those were some pretty simple wishes, and it was irritating the shit out of me that none of them were happening until tomorrow.

"You can use our place while you're there, Hook," Kitty assured him, breaking into my grumpy thoughts. "Just give us a little advance notice so we can get our housekeeper to stock the fridge."

"Are you gonna do the video thing like me and Maylee did?" Bug asked.

"Probably. Hell, she might change her mind. There's no telling. We're not in a rush anyway. She's stuck with me forever and she knows it, marriage certificate or not."

"I'm starving," Chef grumbled. "How long is this shit going to take?"

"Her brother swears that we're all gonna enjoy dinner tonight to make up for that shit they tried to pass off as food last night and then whatever food they're gonna serve after the wedding," I assured them. "They've got some friends from Florida and North Carolina that they've invited, but it's casual, so we don't have to dress up."

"Oh yeah, I met some of them. Had a good chat with a man from North Carolina," Preacher said. "Zeppo and I were talking about Elvis and Tupac and . . ."

"There are so many reasons that those two names aren't even in the same stratosphere," Chef argued. "What the fuck is wrong with you?"

"Well, they do have one major thing in common," Preacher argued.

"What's that?"

"Neither one of them are dead," Preacher scoffed.

"Sweet baby Jesus," Captain whispered as he let his head fall forward and stared at the ground. "I'm afraid to ask. I'm not gonna ask. I don't want to know."

"I believe Elvis changed his name to John Burrows

and became a car salesman in Tacoma."

"And there he goes," Captain said with a sigh.

"Now Zeppo had a pretty good theory about it, and considering his profession, I'm inclined to believe he might be right. He said . . ."

"Here they come," Chef interrupted

I looked toward the doors at the opposite end of the huge room and smiled when I saw the women huddled together. Frankie's niece and nephew were standing with them and seemed to be waiting on something. The first notes to the song started, and I couldn't hold in my laughter as the kids started dancing down the aisle to The Bee Gees' song, "Stayin' Alive."

The girls came down the aisle in the same order as the men beside me. Since Stamp was the last in line, Bernadette was first followed by Pandora, Maylee, and Matalie, who all danced their way down the aisle, making us hoot and cheer.

My sister paused in the doorway and struck a dramatic pose before she started dancing down the aisle toward us as Brea, Jenn, and Paula followed her. Hook nudged my arm and said, "Please tell me those guys are recording this."

"Yep."

"Fantastic," Hook said through his laughter as Paula stopped at the bottom of the steps and turned around to shake her ass at her man, causing all of the women to laugh right along with us.

I looked back to the doorway to find Frankie standing with her arm hooked through her brother Federico's.

"Fuck, that's funny," I heard Kitty shout over the lyrics.

I cheered and then whistled as Frankie and Rico strutted down the aisle to the beat. They got to the bottom of the steps and he twirled her around and then caught her in his arms before he dipped her, laughing right along with her before he pulled her back up and gave her a hug.

Someone cut the music, and Frankie laughed as she walked up the steps toward me. "If I didn't think Bernadette and half the people invited to the wedding would have a stroke, I'd say we do it just like that tomorrow."

"I'm game," I told her.

"We should probably practice with the actual music," the wedding coordinator suggested.

Frankie rolled her eyes and let out a dramatic sigh before she nodded. "Let's go again, girls."

"We'll practice the walk out first then rehearse the entire thing from beginning to end at least once," the woman said as she cued up the music Frankie had chosen.

"And then we'll eat!" Frankie's brother promised. "Most of you seem to be very motivated by food, so that might help."

"What are we eating tonight?" Chef asked.

"I promise, you're gonna love it," was all Rico would say.

"The quicker we get through this, the quicker we can join everyone else for dinner," Bernadette promised.

"It's not too late to fly to Vegas," I whispered as I started escorting Frankie down the steps. "I can book a flight before we even get to those doors back there."

"Don't tempt me, Christopher. That's just cruel."

CHEF

"Now *that's* what I'm talking about," I heard Soda say from the end of the table. "Finally! Some real food."

"Damn, that's good," I heard one of the Ares men say. When I looked in that direction, I saw that Sin, Torpedo, and Executioner were all gnawing on some good Texas-style pork ribs while the rest of our friends talked around them.

I'd already packed away so much food I was afraid I'd pop, but I couldn't resist the bowl of peach cobbler that Brea had set in front of me when she came back to the table.

"This is how people eat in Texas?" Rachel, Zeppo and Ezra Frenkel's sister, asked before she took another bite of her chopped beef sandwich. "This food is delicious."

"We eat this all the time," Brea told her. "As a matter of fact, Tyler, the man that cooked all of this, is from Tenillo. Rico flew him in as a surprise, and he brought in everything he'd need to feed us tonight."

"I can't get enough of . . . well, any of it," another of the group from North Carolina, this one a man named Moshe, said before he took another bite of potato salad. "It's not like anything we have at home."

Brea moaned, and I saw her eyes were closed as she savored a bite of cobbler.

Moshe laughed as he watched Brea enjoy her dessert. "That sound means I need a bowl of that next."

"He's got three different kinds over there. He even brought some Blue Bell ice cream from home," Brea explained. "As far as I'm concerned, that's a state treasure."

"Oh yeah," I agreed. "When I was in prison, I dreamed of Blue Bell."

"I've been curious about that," Moshe admitted.

"The ice cream?" Rachel asked.

"No, we have that locally," Moshe said as he shook his head. He looked thoughtful for a second and then said, "I don't want to overstep, but I understand that your . . . club? That's what it's called, correct? A motorcycle club?"

"Yeah. Time Served Motorcycle Club."

"And yes, all of them have been in prison for one thing or another," Brea said with a grin. She winked at Moshe and added, "Even a few of us women have served time."

"I'm not going to lie," Darragh, one of the men from the Irish group who'd flown up from Florida, said from a few seats away. "When we learned about your group from Rico, I looked into it. Some of your members have very illustrious pasts."

"Illustrious? I like that. Which ones make you say that?" I asked.

"Well, you for one," Darragh admitted. "I remember watching you play football on television when I was a kid."

"You played in the NFL?" Moshe asked.

"I did. I retired because of a knee injury and then moved back to Texas and became a high school science teacher."

"And then you went to prison?" Rachel asked.

"Yes. My wife died, and my daughter got into some trouble before she passed too. I've gotta admit, I wasn't thinking clearly. It wasn't temporary insanity or any kind of bullshit excuse like that. I knew exactly what I was doing when I killed a house full of drug dealers and pimps with a chemical bomb I made at the school one afternoon."

"I think they should have given you a medal instead of incarcerating you," Conor, another of the Irish men, said. "Sounds like you did the world a favor."

I laughed for a second and then nodded. "I think I did."

"Did you kill a house full of drug dealers too?" Rachel asked. Then, realizing what she'd just said, she shook her head and apologized. "I'm sorry. I shouldn't have . . ."

Brea laughed. "It's not a secret. I didn't kill a house full, just one."

"Well, then you need a medal too," Conor asserted.

"The rest of the guys have their own story to tell, but to answer your earlier question, yes, all of the men in my club have been to prison. That's sort of a requirement."

"Not all of the women have," Brea added. "Just a couple of us."

"That's interesting," Rachel said as she looked around the room at the different women.

"You're trying to figure out which ones have, huh?" Brea asked.

Rachel laughed uncomfortably as she looked down at her food. "I was."

"Their histories aren't a secret. I am curious, though. If you had to guess, other than me, which two women would you imagine have been to prison?"

"Hmm," Rachel said as she looked up and studied the women closely before she tilted her head. "The tattooed one."

"Blue. And yes, you're correct. She's an ex-con."

"I know it wasn't Paula because we know her family history," Moshe said as he looked around. "I think it's the one next to Boss. His woman. Jenn, right?"

"Her name is Jenn. Why do you think she's been to prison?"

"She's too nice. She's got to be making amends for something," Darragh said. "I've only talked to her a few times, and she's been perfectly pleasant every time. I think it's her. She's the other one."

"No. She actually owned a software company in Washington state before she moved to Texas and opened a dessert and coffee business. She owns one of the most popular food trucks in town and can cook things that will make you weep with joy," I told them. "Try again."

"That one's too young. So is that one," Rachel said, pointing at August and Sis.

"The one on the right is my daughter, and the other is Captain's daughter," Brea explained.

"It's not Matalie. I talked to her earlier. She's a lawyer," Rachel said. "And Maylee seems too . . . What's the word I'm looking for?"

"She's old money," Moshe said.

"That's it," Rachel agreed. "So it's not her. I'm going to guess that it's Pandora. She's sweet as can be, but I think there's something else there."

"It might be Bernadette," Moshe argued.

"You're both wrong," I told them. "It's the lawyer. She finished college while she was in prison."

"Really?" Rachel asked with wide eyes. "I'd never have guessed!"

"You want to know what she did, don't you?" Brea asked.

"It's killing me not to ask."

Brea told her, "Sometimes, in a relationship, you just want to smack your man in the head with a frying pan. Her man was worse than 99% of them. He was horrible, and she didn't have a way to escape since he was a cop. So after he'd hurt her badly, she shot him in the head with his own gun and then fed him to the gators in Louisiana."

"I think I might be in love," Conor joked. "That's the best thing I've heard all day."

"You just like it because you're from Florida and those things are everywhere," I teased.

"They do come in handy," Conor said with a chuckle. "Those bastards will eat anything."

"Maybe we should tell Hook to be on the lookout for some alligators," I mused. "We could use one or two of them on occasion."

"I'll put in a request," Brea joked. She looked down and realized I'd finished my cobbler, then asked, "Do you want another bowl?"

"I shouldn't."

"But you're going to, aren't you?" Brea asked, knowing me well enough to understand I couldn't pass it up. "Peach again, or do you want to switch it up?"

"I'll come with you," Rachel said. "I'm excited to try this ice cream that you say is so wonderful."

"I'll take cherry if they've got it," I said as I leaned her way. I gave her a quick kiss and then whispered in her ear. "And get me a big bowl of that peach cobbler for us to take back to our room. I think I can think of an even better way to eat it."

"Are we going to make another mess?" Brea whispered in my ear as I nibbled on her neck.

"Damn right, Pickle, and we're going to enjoy the hell out of it."

BLUE

"Okay, so you'll lead, but remember, it's two steps with your left, then one with your right. Just follow along with the beat," I told my new dance partner, Tovah, one of the men from South Carolina who was in business with Frankie's brothers.

"When do we get to the spinning part like they're doing?" he asked, his eyes on August and Rodeo as she did the jitterbug in the middle of the dance floor.

"That's a little bit above your skill level at this point," I teased. "Let's make it around the dance floor at least once, then I'll teach you some of that."

"Okay. I think I've got it. I'm ready when you are," Tovah said with a firm nod. "I'm going to apologize in advance for any injury to your feet that might occur in the next few minutes."

"You're already forgiven," I assured him. "Let's go."

Tovah took a second to gather his courage and then started moving us around the dance floor. He was concentrating so intensely that I couldn't imagine he was having any fun at all, but he was doing really well, so I made sure to tell him so.

"You're very kind," Tovah said with a laugh right before he stepped on my foot again. "I've never really listened to this type of music before, and I've never been to a country bar, so all of this is new to me."

"You're doing great for a first-timer. I promise."

"Have you had fun in New York?"

"I have! It's nothing like the movies, though. I was sure we'd get mugged at least once but nothing. I should have realized that was all dramatization. Look at how they portray Texas most of the time."

"Some of those Texas stereotypes may be true. It's not hard to imagine a few of your family members being involved in a shootout at dusk," Tovah said with a grin.

I laughed along with him and conceded, "I can see why you might think that."

"I might have to visit Texas someday."

"Hit us up if you do. We'll hang out and do Texas things."

"Shootouts in the street?"

"No, mostly cover yourself in bug spray and sit by the fire while you bullshit with your friends and bitch about how hot it was that day."

"We do that at home too. I guess we're not all that different, are we?"

"I don't think we are."

We made it all the way around the dance floor before the song ended, and I grinned at my new friend before I said, "Now you spin your partner once, sort of as a thank you for the dance."

Tovah spun me around, and we laughed as the next song started. As soon as I heard the first notes, I told him, "Jude is about to steal me away."

Tovah was apparently a quick learner because his movements were more smooth than before as he turned us around and moved us along the dance floor, "Why do you say that?"

"May I cut in?" Jude asked from behind me. "I'll swap partners with you."

"Tovah, right?" Pandora asked as she took his hand and stepped in front of him. "I'm Pandora."

"Dance with me, Blue," Jude said as he pulled me into his arms. "This is the first song we ever danced to in your kitchen."

"It's so sweet that you remember," I said honestly. "I told Tovah you were about to cut in."

Jude and I moved in perfect sync after having danced together so many times, even just around our house. He maneuvered us around the other couples on the dance floor, and I couldn't help but laugh as I watched some of the other couples who were just learning. Jude pushed me away and spun me around before he pulled me to him and we got back into rhythm together.

By the time the song changed, I was nearly out of breath. Luckily, it was a waltz with a slower pace, so I had some time to catch my breath.

"I could dance with you all night long, but I suppose we should mingle," Jude said as he looked down at me.

"Not yet. There's nowhere I'd rather be than right here in your arms."

"That's right where you belong, my Blue."

16

BERNADETTE

"Thank you so much for your help today," Maylee told Debbie, the makeup artist we'd used. "You were so kind to put everything on hold while I got my daughter down for a nap. I really appreciate you."

"Are you sure there's nothing else we can do for you before we go and help the others get ready?" Debbie asked as she closed the suitcase that held her hair and makeup supplies.

I looked at the other women, lounging around, their hair and makeup finished early so they could relax before it was time to get dressed for the wedding.

"Frankie wants us to help her get dressed, and then we'll all put our dresses on before we go downstairs," I explained. "You've all been wonderful. Thank you so much."

"It was our pleasure." The rest of her crew who'd been working for a few hours on our hair and makeup nodded in agreement and Debbie continued, "I don't think I've ever had this much fun on a job."

"We're probably not the usual clientele for this hotel," I admitted.

"I can guarantee we're not," Maylee agreed before she

gave them one last goodbye and then walked over to open the door for them.

After they were gone, I stuck my head out to talk to Joe who was standing next to the door and Kyle, standing closer to the elevator. They had been standing in the hall since we got here. "Do you guys need a bottle of water or anything?"

"No, thank you," Kyle answered.

"A pee break? A snack?" I laughed and then asked, "A chair?"

"We're just fine, ma'am," Joe assured me.

"Will you be here all afternoon, or is someone coming to relieve you before we go downstairs?"

"We'll be here. We got word that the nanny will come and get the children in about an hour, and then Lorenzo and Carmine will join us so we can escort all of you downstairs."

"Sounds like a plan. You guys let us know if there's anything you need, okay?"Maylee told them.

"Yes, ma'am."

"It's good that we have a little time," Maylee said as I shut the door. "Boo's been napping for about half an hour, and if the nanny comes down in an hour, that will give her a solid nap."

I walked with Maylee through the small foyer into the living area of the suite and laughed when I looked around. "You're all sitting so still that you look like mannequins."

"Did you see what that woman did to my hair?" Blue asked. "There are so many bobby pins in there that I'm afraid if I turn my head, I'll get stabbed and start bleeding everywhere!"

"But it's beautiful," Maylee tried to reassure her.

"I know! It looks fan-fucking-tastic, but I'm afraid it might be deadly."

"I don't think I've ever looked so glamorous," Paula said as she touched her hair.

"Don't touch it!" Jenn snapped as she grabbed Paula's hand.

"Geez, Mom, don't get your panties in a twist," Paula muttered as she snatched her hand away and dropped it into her lap.

"I'm afraid you might disturb the molecular structure of the shellac they sprayed on there and make a hole if you touch it."

"She's probably already got a big hole," Blue teased.

Paula scoffed. "Whatever. You've got three big holes."

"Three?" Jenn asked with a confused look.

"That mouth of hers is bigger than the Grand Canyon. It's like a black hole that just spouts bullshit day and night."

"Fuck you, tiny person," Blue grumbled.

"Sasquatch."

"Ho bag."

"Skank nugget."

"Twatwaffle."

"Children!" Jenn yelled at the arguing women. "We look like fancy ladies, so let's chill out and use our manners."

"When did you buy Blue manners?" Brea teased.

"I will throw down with you, woman," Blue threatened.

"Bring it, Sasquatch!"

"You're making me cry," Frankie wheezed through her laughter. "If you make my mascara run, I'll kill all three of you."

"Total mafia princess, worried about her makeup," Paula teased.

"I've never had this much makeup on in my life," Frankie said as she fanned her face.

"All of you look beautiful," Maylee assured us.

"Look at my cheekbones!" I exclaimed as I pointed to my face. "Where did those come from?"

"They put some on me too," Pandora said as she stood up and walked over to stand in front of the mirror. She turned around and looked at our friends and said, "We look good. Do you think we could do this at home?"

"I need to scratch my nose, but I'm terrified I'm going to mess something up," Frankie admitted before she started scrunching her face up to move her nose around.

"You only feel like you need to because you can't," Matalie told her. "Scratch the inside of your wrist and get the need to scratch something out of your system. Your nose should stop itching."

Frankie scratched a few times and then looked at Matalie in amazement. "Holy shit. It worked."

"Okay! Let's get back on track. We need to get Frankie into her dress, and then we'll help each other. Brea, you're in charge of pictures."

"Got it," Brea said as she walked across the room and picked up her camera.

"First thing we've got to do is wash our hands to make sure we don't smudge anything on the dress," Jenn reminded everyone.

Everyone got up and spread out around the suite to wash up before they met back in the living room. Once we were all back together, I unzipped the garment bag that was hanging on the end of the curtain rod that went across the terrace windows.

"God, that dress is beautiful, Franks," Paula whispered in awe. "You're really going to be a princess."

"Is her second dress in the other bag?" Pandora asked.

"Yeah. We'll take it down with us when we go. There's a small room attached to the ballroom where we can keep it."

"Are you sure we should get you dressed up here,

Frankie? You'll have to get on the elevator and all that . . ."

"That room is way too small for all of us to get dressed in. We'll do all the major stuff up here and then be really careful going down." Frankie took her robe off and handed it to Paula before she walked to the middle of the room. "This is gonna be quite an undertaking, isn't it?"

"We can handle it," I assured her. "Let me show you. Go pee one more time."

Frankie laughed and took off for the bathroom while I spread the dress out the way the woman at the boutique had shown me. Once Frankie was back, Paula and I helped her step into it, then we pulled it up over her hips as Blue held the bodice up for her to slide her arms into.

"Well that wasn't nearly as painful as I thought it would be," Frankie said with a giggle. "Now I just need the sadist of the bunch to tighten the corset so we can zip this thing."

"While you guys see to that, I'm going to step outside for some air. I can't get any bars on my phone, so I'm going to risk going out onto the balcony so I can call Valentine. I haven't talked to him since I left the room early this morning."

"I'm going with Bernadette," Jenn said as she started walking toward the terrace door. "My phone isn't working well either."

"It's weird," I said as Jenn closed the door behind us. "It's been fine the entire trip, but I found I'd lost service when I checked it a few minutes ago."

"Same. I sent Boss a text 20 minutes ago and got his

answer right after, but now I've got no service at all."

"Still nothing," I said as I leaned against the rail and looked down at the street below. "Man, I'll be so glad when this day is finished."

"I thought you enjoyed planning this sort of stuff."

"I do. But in the future I won't have to be involved in all the activities I plan for an event."

"I just want to wash my face," Jenn complained. She glanced over her shoulder when we heard Boo start crying. She screamed as if she were in pain, and Jenn and I stood, both on high alert since our friends inside the suite were yelling too.

"What the hell?" I barked as I turned to go inside.

"Get over here," Jenn hissed as she yanked on my arm and pushed me against the bricks beside the door. "Listen. There's a man in there. Fuck. Where are the guards?"

"I'm gonna peek in," I said as I slid closer to the door. I used one finger to slide the door open the smallest bit and then ducked down so the couch would hide me if someone happened to be looking out the window. With a quick glance, I could tell there was something horribly wrong. I leaned back against the bricks and whispered, "There's a man holding Boo like a football, and he's got a gun pointed at the girls."

"Holy shit," Jenn whispered. She picked up her phone and shook it as if that would make it work again and then she looked toward the end of the terrace. "We have to get over there and get inside."

"How the fuck are we gonna do that?" I asked.

"I was on that terrace earlier. I'm almost positive I didn't lock the door."

I looked down at the street below us. "I've never been afraid of heights until now."

"Get over it," Jenn hissed as she gauged the distance between us and the terrace next door. "It's like six feet away. We can jump that."

"Right. Yeah. We can do it," I said, trying to reassure myself as I took one more glance toward the door behind us. "We've gotta hurry."

"Okay. We'll climb up on the chair and hold onto the bricks while we stand on the rail, and then we'll just jump over onto that balcony."

"Sure. Okay."

"Calm down, or you're gonna pass out."

"Or I could fall to my death. You know. Whichever happens first."

"I'll go first," Jenn said as she climbed onto the chair. "If I fall, you jump over there and go get help."

"If you fall . . ."

"Not for me. I'll be dead of a fucking heart attack before I hit the ground, I assure you. I can feel one coming on already."

I held my breath as Jenn balanced on the rail and

slapped my hand over my mouth to hold in a scream of terror when she squatted down and jumped toward the balcony next to ours. Her robe flew out behind her like a cape, and it felt like time stood still as she soared through the air. I sucked in a deep breath when she landed on her feet and then rolled forward until she was flat on her back. I heard her moan and gasp for air but didn't waste any more time checking to see if she was okay. She wasn't a splat on the pavement 90 floors down, so if something was wrong with her, it could be fixed.

Before I lost my nerve, I stepped onto the chair and then onto the rail. I had to bite back a screech as I launched myself toward the other balcony and then again when I landed and fell forward, skidding on my knees until I bumped into Jenn.

"Oh fuck. We're not dead."

Jenn groaned as she pushed herself up and then stood. She held her hand out to help me up and winced when she saw my legs. "Shit. You're bleeding."

"But I'm not dead. That's what I'm taking away from this," I said firmly as I reached for the balcony door. "Please be unlocked. Please be . . . Yes!"

Jenn and I ran through the suite, and I bumped into her back when she skidded to a halt in the doorway of the small kitchen. She turned inside and started pulling drawers open and rifling through them. "Look for a knife. Here!"

Jenn held a butcher knife in her hand and handed me a smaller knife.

"Are we just going to walk in and stab him?"

"No. I'm going to stab him from behind. You're going to grab Boo and run for help."

"But . . ."

"Believe me, Bernadette. All the women in that room need is a one-second window of opportunity, and they'll rip that man to shreds."

"Okay. Okay. We can do this."

Jenn nodded. "I'll get him in the arm. You stick this in the back of his thigh right before you grab Boo. Got it?"

"Got it."

Jenn slowly opened the door and peeked out into the hall. "Fuck. There's a man out there I don't recognize, and the guards are gone."

"We'll walk toward the elevator like we don't have a care in the world and take him out."

"God. You already sound like one of the girls," Jenn said with a nervous laugh. "Can you do that? Kill him?"

"Did you hear that baby crying?"

"Alright then. Hide the knife in your sleeve. You go for the soft parts, and I'll go for his neck."

I took a deep breath and gave her a nod. Jenn opened the door and walked out into the hall like she didn't have a care in the world. When we got closer to the man in the hallway, she asked, "Are you a guard?" He didn't say a word, just glared at her. She stepped closer to him and asked, "Is there someone famous in there?"

"Move along."

"There *is* someone famous in there!" Jenn said, excitement in her voice. She stepped closer to him and acted like she was going to lean around him. He turned his body, and without even thinking, I stabbed the knife into the paunch of his stomach and yanked up as hard as I could. He let out a shocked gasp but barely had time to move before Jenn pushed the butcher knife into his throat. He bent forward and made a horrible gurgling sound that just got worse when Jenn yanked the knife out and stepped back to let him fall. He hit his knees, his hands at his throat. Jenn yanked up the back of his jacket, searching for a weapon.

"Found it!" Jenn said as she stepped back with a gun in her hand. "Now remember, grab the baby and run, okay?"

"Got it," I assured her.

"We're gonna have to be quick. Once he hears the door open, he's gonna start to turn, if he's even in the same position he was in before. Shit. I don't know what to do."

"We do what needs to be done, and that's go in there and take care of business. I'll get the baby and take her to safety. What do we do about this guy?" I asked as I looked down at the dead man between us.

"Let him rot."

MATALIE

"Okay, I'm ready," I said as I braced my feet and leaned back, holding Frankie's hands in mine.

"It would be . . ." Blue let out a grunt at the same time Frankie groaned, ". . . easier if I could . . ." There was another grunt and another groan, and I leaned farther back to pull on Frankie since Blue was tugging her the other way. " . . . brace my foot on your ass . . ."

"Enough!" Frankie wheezed.

"Paula! Finger!"

With a wicked giggle, Paula pushed at the back of the corset, and Blue tied off the strings.

"There ya go! Instant skinny!"

"I can't breathe," Frankie gasped.

"Stand up straight and put your shoulders back. Breathe in through your nose and then exhale slowly," Maylee said as I let go of Frankie's hands.

Frankie did as she was told and then asked, "When does it get better?"

"When you take it off," Maylee said with a shrug. "You'll be fine. Oxygen is overrated, and you're going to look fantastic."

From the bedroom, Boo let out an ear-piercing scream, and we turned to look as Maylee darted around Frankie to go to her daughter. She skidded to a stop halfway across the room when a man stepped into the hallway with Boo under his arm. He pointed a gun at Maylee as he yelled, "Get back over there with your girlfriends."

"Give me my daughter," Maylee growled as she stood her ground. The man started to turn the gun toward Boo and Maylee stepped back, never taking her eyes off of the toddler squirming in his hold. She tried to reassure her by saying, "Be still, Boo. Be still," but Boo wasn't having it and just squirmed harder.

"What are you doing, Don?" Frankie asked in a menacing voice.

"Those bastards took my life from me, and I'm going to take it back."

"Let the baby go, and we'll do anything you want," Paula offered.

"You'll do everything I say anyway, Paola. The little girl's going with me, though. I'll give her to your father so he can try again. He fucked up raising the first one, and I think he deserves another chance."

"My father?" Paula asked. I saw her glance toward the bedroom where the man had come from, probably expecting her father to walk out any second now. "How did you get in here?"

"You never heard me come inside over all your cackling. Just shows how unprepared those bastards really are." As he scanned the room, he asked, "Which one of you is Bernadette?"

"She's not here," Frankie told him. I fought the urge to look toward the terrace, wondering if Bernadette and Jenn even realized there was something going on inside.

"Where is she?" the man roared.

"She left," Paula told him with a shrug. "She's who you really want, isn't she?"

"Oh no," the man said with an evil grin. "Your father is outside waiting. He's got plans for you, Paola. Big plans."

"Well, he's fucked then because I'm not going anywhere with either of you old bastards," Paula snapped. "Put the baby down and get out while you can, Don."

"Don't sass me. I won't put up with that shit," the man said as he shifted his weight so he could get a better grip on Boo. "All of you line up. We're going to take a little ride, and then I'm going to send each of you back to your men piece by fucking piece until I run out of bodies to cut up."

"You are way too fucking dramatic," Blue said as she rolled her eyes. "Don't you watch movies? The man who does the long speech always dies."

"Shut up. I'm not the one that's going to die today," the man barked.

"Actually, you are," Blue said as she took a step toward him. From the other side of the room, Brea took a step in his direction, too, causing the man to look from one woman to the other and then back. Since I was on the opposite wall from Brea, I took a step his way, too, splitting his attention three ways now. "You can't shoot all of us at once, and I can guaran-fucking-tee that whoever gets to you is gonna make you regret waking up this morning."

"I'll second that," Brea said as she took another step his way.

I took a step, too, and his gaze wandered over to me.

"Let the baby go and we might let you live."

"No," Blue said, causing the man to look at her now. "I'm going to enjoy killing him."

"Not as much as I will," Paula said as she took a step forward. "Did you think we'd start crying, Don? Are we supposed to be terrified?"

"I'm going to torture you for so long that you won't remember what it's like to live without pain," Maylee said calmly.

"You don't even know who I am, bitch."

"You're the man who threatened my daughter. That's all I need to know."

I saw the door behind him fly open, and there was a split second of confusion as he started to turn around. Boo was yanked backward out of his arm just as he let out a roar of pain. Jenn's head popped up over his shoulder as she planted a knife in the side of his neck causing his gun to thud to the carpet as he fell to his knees. Jenn pressed a pistol to the side of his head as she asked, "Is he alone in here?"

"Boo!" Maylee screamed as she ran past Jenn.

"Shoot him!" Brea yelled.

"No! Let him bleed!" Frankie shouted as she walked closer to him. He coughed and blood sprayed from his mouth, splattering the front of her dress. Frankie didn't even notice as she stepped closer, maintaining eye contact with him the entire time. "Is this the part where you thought I would cry and beg, Don? Surprise. This is the part where *you* cry and beg."

"We should save him," Paula said calmly as she stood beside Frankie. "Give him to the boys and let them play with him for a while before they kill him."

"Make an example out of him. Show him what happens to anyone who messes with our family," Frankie suggested.

"If we're going to keep him alive, we should probably drag the dead guy in from the hallway before someone sees him," Jennifer suggested calmly. "I guess it doesn't matter. Someone's bound to see the blood."

"Shit," Paula hissed as she and Blue squeezed past Jenn to go outside. "Oh! It's my dad. Look at that."

"Oh fuck. I killed Paula's dad?" Jenn whispered.

"She's not gonna hold it against you," Frankie assured her. "You can put the gun down, Jenn. He's about to lose consciousness."

"I vote we shoot him anyway," I said as Pandora walked up beside me. I looked over and saw her eyes were wide with shock, but she nodded. "Pandora's with me. Who else? Majority rules."

"Twist the knife. See what that does," Brea suggested.

"Do not kill him," Maylee ordered from somewhere in the hallway. "Let him suffer."

"Boo's good?" Brea yelled.

"She's okay," Bernadette answered. "This guy isn't

dead."

"Well, shit." Paula sounded genuinely upset to hear he was alive. "I guess we'll drag him inside. Someone needs to go get one of the guys."

"I'm covered in blood," Jenn said. "Oh, Frankie! Your dress!"

"Fuck the dress. Brea, tie him up. Pandora, come help me get out of this goddamn corset before I pass out. Matalie, are you clean? Can you go get the guys?"

"Why the fuck won't my phone work?" I heard Blue yell from the hallway.

"One of them has to have a jammer," Paula answered. "Grab his legs, and let's get him inside."

"Let me in first," Maylee said as she pushed past Paula. "Boo's covered in blood. I need to get her cleaned up. If Enzo sees her like this, he'll set this whole town on fire."

"I'm clean. I'll go," I said as I skirted past the girls and walked out into the hall, making sure to tiptoe around the blood. I stopped and looked down at the man on the floor and realized he was breathing shallowly. Blood was still trickling out of the wound on his stomach as well as the one on his neck.

"Frankie, wash your face. You've got blood on it," I heard Pandora say.

"No. I don't want to ruin my wedding hair."

"We're not having a fucking wedding today, Frankie," Blue said as she picked up Paula's dad's foot and pulled. "Help me out here, Paula. He's not exactly a lightweight.

"We *will* have a wedding," Frankie said firmly. "They came here today to stop it from happening, and anyone that's working with them needs to see that they didn't win. The wedding is on."

"Well, shit," Paula grumbled as she bent down and grabbed the other foot. "I really wanted to get all these fucking pins out of my hair."

While I waited on the elevator, I watched them drag the man into the suite but got confused when Paula yelled, "Jenn! They're playing our song!"

I burst out in hysterical laughter when I heard Jenn yell, *"You can do it, put your ass into it!"*

I was still laughing when I walked out of the elevator.

17

CAPTAIN

"Doesn't he seem really calm for a man who's about to get fitted with a ball and chain?" Soda asked.

"It's hard to be anything other than calm when you've got a kid sleeping on you," I pointed out. "Look at him. He's even drooling."

"How that boy can sleep in a crowd of people is beyond me," Chef said from my other side.

"You didn't sleep in prison?"

"I did but never well," Chef admitted. "I had a cellmate who snored like a buzzsaw. Sometimes I'd lay awake at night and plan his death."

"You should hear Blue. Funny thing is she doesn't believe me when I tell her she snores."

"She always has," Santa agreed from his chair across from us. "It's hard to believe Chef and Brea can't hear her at their house."

"I swear, one of these days I'm going to record her just so I can prove it," Preacher threatened.

Rodeo walked back into the room with his phone in his hand and I asked, "How are your girls doing?"

"Still the cutest babies in the state of Texas," Rodeo boasted.

"Hey now!" Bug piped up from his spot in front of the television.

"Your girl holds that title right along with them," Rodeo assured him. "Stamp, your kids are out in the hall with Paula's."

"Good," Stamp yelled from the kitchen.

"What time do you think we should start getting dressed?" Hook asked. "We've got an hour before we're supposed to meet downstairs."

"Frankie suggested we take it in shifts. Bernadette even wrote down a schedule," Santa said, motioning toward the table where Bug, Kitty, and Boss were playing cards with Paula's brothers, Vincente and Antonio, and Frankie's brother, Ziggy. "They're keeping score on the back of it since that's the only paper we could find."

"How are they doing, Boss?" Preacher asked.

Boss looked over at Preacher with a disgusted look as he shook his head. "No hope for 'em."

"Hey! I'm working on it!" Antonio argued. "I've never played Spades before."

"We need to find some dominos," Rodeo suggested. "I would school them on some bones."

The door opened and Paula and Stamp's sons walked into the suite. After they'd greeted everyone, they stood around the table watching the card game, asking questions about how to play.

"I want to go home," Preacher whined. "I miss my bed. I miss my porch. Hell, I even miss having Mouth show up at the crack of dawn while she talks shit over coffee."

"Hey now," Chef grumbled half-heartedly, never opening his eyes as he reclined on the couch with his feet propped up on the table.

"I've got a question, Santa."

"What's up, Cap?" Santa asked.

"Where the hell is Hammer, and why isn't he going to be in the wedding?"

"He's going to be an usher," Santa said with a shrug. "He told me he wasn't sure he'd be able to come to New York, so he didn't want to agree to be in the wedding and then have to back out."

"Is he still on parole?" Soda asked.

"No. He's been free and clear for a while," Boss said from the table.

"So I made him an usher with the other guys. That way, if he didn't show, it wouldn't make that much of a difference in the long run," Santa explained.

"Shouldn't he be here now?" Preacher asked.

"I got a text from him earlier that said he'd be here in just a bit. I'm not sure where he took off to this morning."

"Matalie? What's wrong?" I heard Boss say. Out of

the corner of my eye, I saw him push his chair back from the table and stand as I did the same.

When I turned around, I saw Matalie standing at the mouth of the hallway. She was wearing a robe and no shoes with her hair in an elaborate updo and more makeup than I'd ever seen on her

"What's going on?" I asked as I rushed around the couch toward her.

Matalie put her hands up and looked around the room for a second before she said, "First, let me say that everyone is fine. No one is hurt, but we need some . . . help."

"What the fuck is going on?" Boss barked.

Matalie tilted her head toward Paula's brothers and son as she bit her lip. "Can we talk alone?"

"Is that blood?" I asked when I got closer and noticed the small dark flecks splattered across her chest.

Matalie's eyes got wide, and she tilted her head toward the Morettis and Campanas again before giving me a pointed look.

"Sweetheart, we're in their house right now. Whatever happened is going to involve them anyway," I murmured as I stared into her face. "Talk to me. Where did the blood come from?"

Matalie clutched the front of my shirt. She pulled me closer to her and whispered, "They might be upset. We killed Paula's dad and some other guy, and we need your help."

I felt my head jerk back and turned around to look at

Boss in confusion before I shrugged my shoulders.

"My girls are down there," Bug said as he brushed past us and rushed toward the door.

"They're fine, Bug. I promise."

"What the fuck happened?" Boss barked.

I looked over at Vincente and then his brother Antonio before I said, "There was a problem with your father and . . ."

"What the fuck is that bastard doing here?" Antonio barked as he stood up. "I'll kill him if he's done something . . ."

"We already did that," Matalie said before she bit her lip, showing her discomfort. "Well, almost. He was still breathing when I came downstairs."

"What?" Vincente yelled as he walked toward us. I turned around and faced him, blocking Matalie from his view, as my brothers crowded around us to help me protect my woman. "Did he hurt anyone? How did he get in? Where the fuck are the guards? Are the women okay?"

"None of us were hurt, but we don't really know how to . . . We brought the bodies . . . "

"Bodies?" Boss yelled.

"Just two," Matalie said quickly. "All of you need to calm down. Everyone is just fine. Frankie insists the wedding is still on, and from the tone of her voice, anyone that wants to argue with her will end up dead. That means you need to stay down here and get dressed so we're not late."

"What in the fuck?" Santa asked. When I looked at him, I saw Jared was still sleeping on his chest even though Santa was standing now.

"Give me my son," Kitty said as he took Jared out of Santa's arms. "Matalie, you're sure Pandora's okay?"

"I'm positive."

"I'm going to check on our girls then," Kitty said.

"Rodeo, Soda, you're with Kitty. Stay with the girls until we get in touch with you," Boss ordered. The men rushed out the door, and Boss turned around and looked at the Morettis.

"We'll go upstairs with you," Vincente said as his brother Antonio stood behind him.

"We're taking the stairs," Luca said as he, Matteo, and Zach walked toward the door.

"I'm serious about what Frankie said. This wedding is happening. I promise your women are fine. You'll see them all dressed up in less than an hour," Matalie assured my brothers. She looked at the clock on the wall and winced. "We've got 25 minutes before we're supposed to be downstairs. All of you need to get dressed, and we'll see you then."

"I want to see Frankie," Santa growled.

"No! She made you spend last night alone so you didn't see her the day of the wedding, and you're not going to fuck that up by going up there now. There are traditions in place, Santa," Matalie argued. "Please just get dressed, and

I'll go upstairs with the . . . non-MC family."

"My Blue's okay?"

Matalie laughed softly and assured him, "Blue is fine. So is Brea. Jenn and Bernadette saved our asses. Maylee's got Boo now . . ."

"Oh shit," Santa whispered.

"I'm pretty sure that Maylee and Bug are not going to make the ceremony," Matalie said with a wince. "Boo's not hurt, but it's gonna take some time for Maylee to calm down."

"What happened?"

"While we were distracted, a man came into the suite and took Boo from the bedroom and then held a gun on us. He threatened to hurt Boo but didn't get a chance. I'm sure Maylee isn't going to want her out of her sight for a while. Or ever." Suddenly, the room was filled with different ringtones, and everyone jumped. "They must have figured out how those assholes jammed the cell phone signals. Make your calls quick and get dressed. I'll go upstairs with these guys."

"Are you sure you're okay?" I asked Matalie. I reached up and rubbed my thumb over a spot of blood on her face. "Even covered in blood, you're still beautiful."

"Thanks," Matalie said with a grin. "You think this is bad, you should see Frankie's wedding gown."

"Shit," I whispered.

"I'm okay, Gus. I promise."

"We'll take care of her and the rest of the women

ourselves," Vincente assured me, talking a little louder than before so he could be heard over all the men who were now talking on their phones.

"Boss, she's fine, but I think you might want to come talk to Jenn for a minute," Matalie said as she touched my friend's arm. "You should bring Stamp too. They might need a . . . moment."

Boss stared at Matalie and then nodded before he said, "I'll get him, and we'll follow you up."

"You get dressed. I'll see you at the wedding."

"Are you sure, babe?"

"I didn't lift a finger today, so I'm fine. Believe me." Matalie laughed uncomfortably and then said, "I mean, you learn something new every day right? I had no idea Jenn was into knife play."

I barked out a laugh, and Matalie grinned at me. "We did have Brea tie the guy up, so all that kinky shit she and Chef are into has really come in handy."

"Jesus. No wonder all of you get along so well with my sister," Antonio said through his laughter. "Let's go figure this shit out and get Frankie and Santa married so we can send you back to the relative safety of your lives in Texas."

I gave Matalie a kiss before she turned to walk away with the men.

"Yeah," Boss scoffed. "As if location affects their body count."

Matalie shot Boss a toothy grin over her shoulder and replied, "Hey! A girl's gotta do what a girl's gotta do."

"I'll watch out for her, man," Stamp said as he walked past me. "Tell Santa we'll be back as quickly as we can."

"Will do."

"Alright, everyone!" Santa shouted so everyone would look his way. He held his phone up and said, "Big City says that come hell or high water, we're having a fucking wedding today, so I need all of you to put on your monkey suits. We're going to be cutting it close to the wire, but apparently, she doesn't mind making a grand entrance."

"Fuck. Surely dead bodies are reason enough not to have to wear that fucking tux," Preacher grumbled.

"You fuck up my girl's big day by bitching, and I'll add another dead body to the pile," Santa threatened.

"Bitch, try me," Preacher growled.

"Children!" Chef yelled. "Shut up and focus. We've got a wedding to get to!"

"Fuck. He's starting to sound like Boss," I heard Preacher mumble before he started flipping through the garment bags that were hung on a rack by the wall. "That's the last thing we need: a salt and pepper set yelling at us all the time."

There was laughter, but it wasn't as exuberant as it usually was, probably because we were all worried about what was going on in the suite above us.

PAULA

Blue dropped my father's foot, and it hit the carpet with a thump. She rested her hands on her knees and tried to catch her breath. "Shit. I need to start working out more."

"It's not that often you work up a sweat hauling around a dead body, but you did a great job," Pandora said as she stared down at my father's face. "You must look like your mom, Paula."

"I do, thank God."

"Should we put him in the bathroom?" Brea asked.

"No, Maylee's in that one getting Boo cleaned up. We'll leave him right here. They're gonna have to replace the carpet anyway," Frankie said as she studied the men on the floor. "That's Stamp's uncle. It's been ages since I've seen the man, and the years haven't been good to him."

"Is he dead?" Pandora asked.

"Oh yeah. He's most definitely dead," Frankie said. "He couldn't live for more than a second or two after that kind of injury. The amount of blood on my dress is more than enough to have made his heart stop, and there's even more around him on the floor."

"What are we going to do?" Brea asked. "It's not like we can bury them somewhere."

"We could stuff them in some luggage and leave them in Central Park," Jenn suggested.

"I'm sure that the guys will call my brothers and . . ." I started to say just as the lock on the door clicked and someone pushed it open. It hit Stamp's uncle in the head, and I couldn't help but giggle right along with Jenn, remembering our first adventure in crime. It thumped against his head again and then Bug stuck his head in through the gap and looked down. "Well, that'll do it."

"Are your brothers gonna be pissed?" Jenn whispered.

"Believe me, they'll be fine with it," I assured her. "Grab his leg, Blue. We've gotta drag him in a little farther so Bug can come inside."

The two of us grunted as we pulled him a couple of feet farther into the hallway. In unison, we dropped his feet, and it didn't bother me at all when I heard him moan.

"Where is she?" Bug asked as he walked inside. He didn't once glance down at the men.

I pointed toward the bathroom, and he pushed past me to find Maylee and their little girl.

"Are you serious about going through with the wedding, Frankie?" Bernadette asked from the kitchen where she was drying her hands after scrubbing off the blood that had covered them after she'd stabbed the man in the thigh.

"What's she going to wear?" Jenn asked. "Look at her."

"She can wear the second dress that she got for the reception. It's not as elaborate as that one, but it doesn't have any blood on it either."

"That's perfect!" I agreed.

Jenn nodded. "It's beautiful too."

"They're right," Brea told Frankie. "It's perfect."

"Well, Frankie, if we're doing this, we need to help you get changed and see if we can salvage your makeup."

"You know the best part?" Frankie asked as she started walking toward the bedroom to change. "That other dress doesn't have a fucking corset."

The door opened again, and my brothers walked into the suite.

"Paola, are you okay?" Vincente asked as he pushed the door open just enough to get inside. Antonio followed him, and they both stopped and looked down at the bodies in front of them. "That's Don Russo."

"I thought that was him," Frankie said from behind me. My brothers looked over my shoulder at her, and their eyes grew wide. "I'm not hurt. It was arterial spray from one of their neck wounds. I'm going to change. Paula, if you can leave them to that, you need to get dressed."

"She's going to go through with it?" Vincente asked as the door opened again, and Boss and Stamp walked in.

"One of the girls suggested she postpone it, and she gave that a hard pass. This is happening now more than ever. I think she's pissed and has a point to make." I put my hand up so Boss and Stamp didn't come any farther. "Wait a sec, you guys. The girls are probably not all decent. Not that they ever are, but you get what I mean. I'll grab your women, and you can talk to them here in the living room."

"They're okay?" Antonio asked.

"They just went two rounds with the mafia, Antonio. They're a little testy."

"Fuck. We should have killed him to start with, but I just thought . . ."

"That's your father, isn't it?" Stamp asked as he stared at the men on the floor. "And there's dear old Uncle Don. I guess they put their differences aside for the day."

"I want to know where the fuck the guards were while this was happening," Boss said angrily. "We were promised that the women had protection!"

Vincente was looking at his phone, and as he slipped it into his pocket, he shook his head. "They're dead in the stairwell. Zach and the Russo boys are collecting them. We'll take care of this shit."

"I have to get dressed," I told them. "I'll send Bernadette and Jenn out, but you need to be in tuxes within the next 20 minutes or Bridezilla will start tearing the place up."

"It's like nothing happened," Bug said as he walked out of the hall bathroom with Boo in his arms. She was in a diaper and her hair was wet from the bath, but she looked perfectly normal. I reached out and booped her nose, and the little girl giggled. "Maylee's shaken up, but she insists that she's going to be with Frankie as long as Boo can stay with one of us through the wedding."

"Give her to Hammer. He won't be on stage, and Boo adores him," I heard Stamp suggest as I walked into the master bedroom.

I shut the door behind me and looked around the room. "Where are Jenn and Bernadette? Boss and Stamp want to talk to them."

"They're in the guest bathroom cleaning up."

I stuck my head out into the hall and told the guys where their women were and then hurried back to join the chaos. Brea stepped in front of me and studied my face. "There's no blood on you, so you should be good to help Frankie. I'll get my dress on and then relieve you so you can get dressed too."

"This is one fucked-up day," I whispered. "Is Frankie okay?"

"She's handling it like any good mafia princess would."

"Pissed off and calling for someone's head?" I asked.

Brea laughed as she nodded. "That's exactly what she's doing."

18

JENN

"You've got to wash it or you'll never get the rocks and dirt out," Blue was sitting on the edge of the tub with her phone in her hand and feet in the water as she watched Bernadette use a washcloth to pat the scrapes on her knees.

"I *am* washing it," Bernadette argued as she gently dabbed at the blood. "What does it look like I'm doing?"

"Being a pussy," Blue said as she set her phone on the back of the toilet. "I sent a text to Sis, and she's finding us some bandages to wrap your legs with. She'll be up in just a few minutes."

"She's helping August get the kids ready, isn't she?"

"August is doing the little girl's hair, so she's going to stay with them while Sis finds what we need."

"I'm all cleaned up, and I think the bleeding has stopped," I said as I lifted the towel off my knee and looked at the scrape I'd gotten from the concrete.

Someone tapped on the door, and I heard Boss ask, "Are y'all decent?"

I glanced over at the others and saw that they were both covered before I opened the door. Boss rushed in and pulled me into his arms as Stamp walked past us to get to the bathtub.

Blue and Bernadette's argument was drowned out when Boss crushed me to his chest and started whispering in my ear. "I was so fucking terrified, baby. What happened?"

"We were on the terrace when they came in, so we went next door and . . ."

"The terraces are connected up here?"

"No. We jumped."

Boss grabbed my shoulders and pushed me away from him as he stared into my face. "You what?"

"We jumped from one to the other and . . ."

"Do you know how high up we are?"

"Obviously," I said, exasperated now. "Don't chew me out."

"You could have died!"

"He had a gun . . . I had to do something!"

"Stay on the fucking terrace and call for backup! That's what you should have done!"

"Don't you dare yell at me. I've had a rough fucking day," I shouted back. "I have so much makeup on that if I blink wrong, it will go everywhere. If you make me cry I will . . . I'll stab you dead. And you won't be the first one I've taken out today."

"Oh, sweetheart," Boss whispered as he pulled me back into his arms.

I felt his arm move and hissed, "Don't touch my hair and don't make me cry. You're being too nice. Start yelling again."

Boss chuckled, and I knew that he was smiling as he rubbed his hands up and down my back. "You saved Boo and our friends, Jenn."

"I was so scared. When I saw him holding the baby, I didn't give a shit how high up we were. I had to do something."

"I am washing it, goddammit!" Bernadette yelled.

I lifted my head off of Boss's chest and looked over at the tub. Bernadette was glaring at Blue, and Stamp was standing off to the side, watching the drama unfold.

"Obviously, you never skinned your knee as a child. I can see little bits of rock and dirt in there, Bernadette. I'm just trying to help you."

"It hurts!"

"Well it's gonna hurt worse when you get gangrene and your fucking leg rots off!"

"I hate to say this, Birdie, but Blue's right. You're not really doing anything by patting it. You need to let her scrub it."

Bernadette glared at Stamp. "But it hurts!"

"Stop being a pussy! Half an hour ago, you stabbed two men, and now you're squeamish about a boo boo?"

"I'll stab you next!"

"Let me help you!" Blue screamed as she stood up and got in Bernadette's face. "I couldn't do anything out there, but I can do this. Let me fix it!"

"You're going to make me cry," Bernadette whispered as her face fell.

"Don't you dare fuck up your face. Frankie will kill us both."

"My friends are certifiable," I whispered to Boss. "I better wade in there before someone else gets hurt."

"Are you sure you're okay?"

"I'm not going to think about it right now because Blue's right. If I walk down the aisle with mascara running down my face, Frankie will kick my ass. We've got to hold our shit together for the next hour or so and then we can all have the breakdown we deserve."

"You're serious?"

"I am dead serious. If I think about it right now, I'll probably throw up. I pulled a Spider-Man 90 stories above the ground and lived to talk about it. I'm going to focus on that right now rather than . . . the rest."

"After the wedding . . ."

"After the wedding, I'm going to lose my shit. I have it scheduled. I haven't cleared it with Bernadette yet, but she's probably going to do the same thing as soon as the photographer's finished with us."

"I heard that!" Bernadette said as she walked past us toward the sink. "Come hold my hand, Peter Parker. Blue's about to make me cry."

"No crying!" I snapped.

"I'm not crying right now, but after the ceremony, I'm gonna completely come unglued."

"In a few hours, we're all gonna get shitty, sloppy drunk, and there's nothing anyone can do about it," Blue said firmly. "We deserve it."

"I wonder how many edibles Paula has left?" I asked as I watched Bernadette sit on the vanity. Blue turned the water on and tested the temperature. When it was ready, Bernadette spun around and put her feet in the sink. Stamp came over and held her hands, and I winced when Blue used a cup to pour water over Bernadette's legs. I started to get a little queasy, so I hugged Boss one more time and then made my excuses. "I'm going to get dressed and check on everyone else. I'll send Sis in here when she comes up."

"Are you okay, Jenn?" Blue asked through our reflection in the mirror. "Really okay?"

"I'll be fine. It's not my first rodeo, remember?"

"That doesn't make it any easier, though, does it?"

"When I start to doubt myself, all I have to do is remember how terrified Boo sounded while he was holding her."

Blue laughed, but there was no joy in it. "When I think about that, I want to revive the son of a bitch and then kill him myself."

"I'm pretty sure Maylee's already got that arranged."

Bernadette laughed. "And I'm not even gonna complain when she doesn't run it by me."

BUG

"Little Bunny Foo Foo hopping through the forest, scooping up the field mice and bopping them on the head," Hammer sang from where he was sitting on the couch entertaining my daughter. Boo's laughter was like a balm to my soul, and the only thing that could pull me back from the ledge I was standing on. I wanted to find anyone who was involved with what happened earlier and rip them limb from limb before I tortured them with fire until they were just a shell of the person they'd been.

"You okay, man? You look . . . homicidal," Captain said as he straightened my bow tie. When he was finished, he motioned toward his own tie and asked, "Am I straight?"

"You're good," I assured him. "And I'm alright. Boo's already forgotten about it, and Maylee's . . . coping, so I'm fine."

"Do we need to find you an abandoned building somewhere?" Boss asked as he walked over to us. I reached out and adjusted his bow tie before I shrugged. "It might help, but I can think of other things that might help more."

"When he says he's fine, it kind of reminds me of the tone of voice Matalie uses when she's really *not* fine at all."

I laughed at Captain and agreed, "I know that tone, and you might be right. Inside, I'm . . . churning. When I think of how much danger my little girl was in and not being there to help her, my guts get all twisted and my heart starts racing."

"I can't believe Frankie is insisting we go through with all of this," Captain said with a glance over at Santa who wasn't in much better shape than me.

We turned toward the door when it opened and watched Zach, Luca, and Matteo come into the suite. They looked tense, and I could only imagine what was going through their heads. I was shocked when they came our way rather than rush to the bedroom to get dressed.

"Bug, I want to apologize for what happened," Zach started. I shook my head, and he put his hand up to stop me from saying anything. "We thought we had this taken care of, and we were wrong."

"We thought by keeping the old men alive, it would show good will to the rest of the organization, and we were wrong," Matteo conceded.

"My grandfather is dead, but their uncle is holding on for now. We'd give you and your men the opportunity to take care of business, to try and make up for what happened with your women, but there's no way he's going to make it long enough for us to get through this wedding and get to him."

I nodded at Zach and asked, "Is he in pain?"

"He's conscious and gasping for air. Somehow, he's still functioning even after Jenn hit all the major parts and lost nearly all of his blood," Luca explained. "I have no fucking idea how the man is still alive."

"I'm not sure either. The carpet was absolutely saturated," Boss said.

"They bled out inside the suite?" Captain asked.

"In the foyer," Boss clarified.

"How are the women going to get out without getting blood all over them?"

Luca let out a nervous laugh at Captain's question, and his brother said, "We got some plastic tarps from maintenance. They'll be able to get out of the room and down the hall to dry carpet without ever touching any blood. We checked on them before we came down, and Sis was bandaging Bernadette and Jenn. They're the only two that weren't dressed."

"It shouldn't take them long then," I mused as I looked at my watch.

"Rodeo and Soda are already downstairs on usher duty. We'll get dressed really quick and join them. Bernadette said the wedding is going to start 20 minutes late, and if anyone has a problem with it, she's going to unleash Frankie on their ass," Zach told us with a grin. "I swear, when I talked to her earlier, it was like having a conversation with her brothers. She had that same fire in her eyes that Rico, Ziggy, and Relio get when they're pissed."

"Is everyone decent?" I heard Sis call out from the doorway. There was a chorus of "Yes!" from around the room. "I'm here to get you all herded downstairs."

"How are the girls?" Stamp asked as he finished tying his shoes.

"They're good. We got Jenn and Bernadette bandaged up, and they're already dressed," Sis explained. "I just got off the phone with August, and she's taking Freddy and Olivia down now."

"Zach, Luca, and Matteo are getting dressed. It shouldn't take them long at all," Boss explained.

"Okay, good. All of you look dashing, but I promised Bernadette I'd do a quick inspection, so line up and let me look at ya," Sis said as she motioned toward the door.

"We're grown men, you know. We can dress ourselves," Kitty argued.

"Your tie is crooked, and you have crumbs in your beard," Sis snapped. "Line up."

"God, she's just as bossy as her mama," Preacher grumbled as he walked toward the door. "She used to be such a sweet little girl and now . . ."

"She's a sweet young woman," Chef growled.

"Since y'all are leaving, I'm going to take Boo downstairs and hang out with Jared," Hammer said as he stopped in front of me so I could kiss my little girl. "I think I'm gonna teach them a few songs, maybe even see if they can pick up a dance routine or two while you guys are busy."

"Do not corrupt the children," Preacher warned. "Bug, are you sure he's trustworthy to be around your kid? Kitty? Come on!"

"This coming from a man who taught my son to check for listening devices in our house," Kitty said drolly.

"You did that?" Captain asked.

"He did," Sis answered as she slowly shook her head. She walked from one man to the next, adjusting ties and smoothing lapels until she got to Chef. She looked up at him and smiled. "You're the handsomest man in this room."

"In this state," Chef argued with a grin.

"No, my man is downstairs. He's the handsomest guy in the state. You win this room."

"Burn," Chef said before he leaned down and kissed her cheek.

"Okay, we're ready!" Luca said as he walked out of the bedroom and sighed. "Check me out, pretty lady."

"You should hang out with your dad more so you can learn to be a little more . . . suave," Sis suggested.

"She thinks I'm cooler than you," Stamp teased his son.

"I didn't say you were cool, I just think you're cooler than him," Sis argued.

"Damn, the girl is on fire today," I joked. I nudged Preacher with my elbow. "Get it? I made a fire joke."

Preacher rolled his eyes as Sis said, "You all look very dashing in your tuxedos. Now I'm going to go find August and take our seats before the festivities start."

"Wave bye to Daddy, Boo Boo," Hammer said from the doorway. I blew my daughter a kiss, and she blew one back before Hammer said, "I'll take care of her, Bug. She'll be fine. I promise."

"Thanks, brother."

"Anytime, my friend."

19

SANTA

"I can't believe we're going through with this," I muttered as I paced back and forth in front of the doorway that would lead us out to the ballroom for the ceremony. "We should scrap this shit and go the fuck home before anything else happens."

"Paula said Frankie's determined to go through with everything as planned. She went off about family responsibility and not showing any weakness, but all I could think about was how close I came to losing her today," Hook admitted. He looked at his shoes and shook his head sadly. "I know we've all been through some hairy shit at home, but what happened today hit me hard for some reason."

"It's because Boo was involved," Preacher said. "We know our women can get through anything, but the entire dynamic of our club . . . our family . . . has changed. We've got little ones around now and grandkids popping up left and right. Since most of us have never had kids, it's thrown us off our game."

"That's harsh," Captain said.

"It's true, though. They've changed our world. Our priorities are completely different now. Before I got with Blue, I was just sort of coasting along. Now I have her on the forefront of my mind, even when she's just fine. If she doesn't pick up the phone, I worry something has happened. If she gets a cough, I'm terrified that she's gonna get sick and I'm going to lose her. Then you add in the teenage girls, and I worry about every awful thing that could happen as they get older and branch out on their own. And then there's Jared. What if he sees us doing shit that fucks him up somehow and *he* ends up in prison? And little Boo. She looks at me like I've got the world on a fucking string, and that's a lot to live up to. Now we've got babies who depend on us to keep them safe and happy. It's so much more than I ever thought I'd have in life, and the thought of anything happening to *any* of them scares me to death."

"Before Matalie and August, all I had to worry about was Mom. I didn't even have a fucking dog to take care of. Now I've got my old lady, my daughter, fucking Rodeo . . . Add the babies to that, and I'm surprised I don't have an ulcer."

"I'm right there with you, Captain. My old lady is terrified of heights, and she jumped from one balcony to another to protect her friends. I love all your women, but I'm so pissed at her for putting herself in danger that I want to shake her till her teeth rattle, but I can't. I'd do the same for any one of you," Boss admitted.

"I want to bring something to the table for a club vote," Kitty piped up.

"Now?" Boss asked him.

"Yeah, now," Kitty snapped. "I just can't . . . What if something had happened up there? We wouldn't have even known until they were late to the wedding. And Boo . . . Fuck. That could have been one of my kids. I don't know how Bug's still standing."

"It's taken effort," Bug admitted. "Boo and Jared are with Hammer, and your girls are in the congregation with their new friends who all have their own personal bodyguards. That's all that's keeping me here right now. I want to yank Boo up and hold her tight while I sweep Maylee off to the airport so we can board the next flight home. I want to lock all of us in the house for . . . well, probably forever, to be honest. I can't even . . . I just can't even wrap my head around . . . Fuck."

"That settles it," Kitty said with a firm nod. "I'm putting it to a vote. I propose that when we get home, we get Rodeo and his crew to dig a moat around our properties. We'll put up walls, razor wire, and get the Ares men to help us figure out some tripwires and landmines."

"I'll wrangle some gators from my swamp property and put them in the moat. We'll take shifts, four at a time with a man on each corner," Preacher interrupted. "No one comes in who's not been vetted."

"We'll make a list of approved people," Kitty suggested. "All of us, the Ares men and women, Pop, and . . . that's it. No one else."

Boss dropped his head and stared at his shoes. "Apparently, Preacher's converted Kitty. If Hammer's in one of your heads and someone starts singing, I'll shoot myself."

"Well, I guess it would be nice if I could touch your body. I know not everybody has got a body like you . . ." Chef sang as he started dancing.

"But I've gotta think twice before I give my heart away and

I know all the games you play . . ." Captain, Kitty, and Stamp joined in as they snapped and danced along with him.

"What the fuck? I'm gonna . . ." Boss fumed. "No! Just . . ."

"*Maybe* . . ." Preacher threw his head back and sang along, and I thought Boss was going to have a stroke.

"Oh shit. Oh shit," Hook kept chanting through his laughter. "Oh God."

"So fucked up," Bug gasped. "Holy shit."

I heard someone behind me snort, and when I turned around, I realized that the videographer was standing behind me with his camera aimed at my friends. I lost it. For the rest of our lives, this day was going to live in mine and Frankie's hearts forever, but with this added bonus, we'd never get tired of watching our big day play out.

"*Gotta have faith* . . ." they sang as they danced. Horribly, I might add.

"I've seen a lot of shit in my life, but never anything like this," I heard Rico, Frankie's brother, say.

His brother Ziggy was laughing so hard he had tears on his face, but Relio looked stunned as he said, "I'm so confused. What is happening right now?"

Hook was gasping for air, bent over with his hands on his knees as he wheezed out an occasional cackle. I was laughing so hard that my sides hurt, and Bug was leaning against Hook as he, too, tried to catch his breath.

"Oh fuck," Bug muttered. "I just can't take it."

Boss never even cracked a smile. He just stood there with a murderous expression as everyone around him lost their fucking minds.

"Are you done?" He asked as he glared at all of us. Finally, he looked at Rico and asked, "Do you have problems like this?"

Rico was laughing too hard to answer, and Ziggy was making a wheezing sound as he clutched his stomach. Relio's head was tilted to the side, as if he were wondering what sort of alternate universe he'd found, and the poor videographer could barely hold his camera still.

"Every one of you is fucking dead to me," Boss growled as he put his hands up and then let them fall. "When we get back to Texas, I'm going to start a new club. Once I get it established, we're gonna come after all of you and just . . . wreak havoc."

But my friends weren't finished trying to lighten the mood as the song wound down. All of them were laughing, too, as they stood next to each other and took a dramatic bow for their audience. It was so funny that Boss smirked a little. When Captain did a passable Elvis impersonation and said, "Thank you. Thank you very much," Boss lost it and laughed right along with the rest of us.

What had started out as a stressful, terrifying afternoon had turned into one of the funniest things I'd ever seen and something I'd never forget, especially since it was on video.

I couldn't wait to show Frankie, and by the time I got the chance to, she'd be my wife.

FRANKIE

"You look stunning, Frankie," Paula said as she adjusted my necklace. "How are you?"

I considered lying but knew that if any of my friends could understand what I was thinking, it would be Paula. "I'm wondering if I should call this off and try again another day."

"Try what again?"

"The wedding."

"Why?"

"We got held at gunpoint an hour before I'm supposed to walk down the aisle, and my wedding gown was covered in blood. If that's not a bad omen, I don't know what is."

Paula bit her lip as she looked out the window behind me. After a few seconds, she said, "I think it was fate that you chose two gowns. You didn't *need* the one you're wearing right now. Most brides just wear their gown to the reception and bustle the train, but you were being extra and had to have a wardrobe change. I think everything happened just the way it was supposed to."

"But Boo and . . . and then Jenn and Bernadette . . ." I took a deep breath and blew it out slowly as I blinked rapidly, trying not to cry. "I just don't know if I can do this today. I don't know if I should."

"I was hoping the vengeful anger wouldn't dissipate until after the reception or at least until after the wedding," Paula said before she sighed. "Now here's the real question of the hour. Do you need me to be sympathetic to your feelings like we've learned to be, or do you need me to be the girl that grew up in this life?"

I thought about it for a second and then took a deep breath as I squared my shoulders and lifted my chin. "Be the girl that grew up like this."

"Okay. You asked for it," Paula warned. I nodded, and in the next second, her face changed into an angry mask and her voice was harsh and angry. "Francesca, this day is not about you. This day is about your family, and how you proceed in the next few hours is going to reflect on them. You will dry your eyes and focus on what needs to be done. You *will* walk down that aisle to your intended with your shoulders back and your head held high. And you *will* have a smile on your face while you do it."

I nodded and glanced over Paula's shoulder at Matalie and Jenn who were staring at us in shock. They didn't understand the life we'd come from, and I prayed that they never would, but that little pep talk from Paula was working perfectly to get my mind where it needed to be.

"There is more riding on this day than your delicate feelings, Francesca. You need to keep that in mind and move forward. What happened before was collateral damage that doesn't mean a fucking thing in the long run. Boo is fine. We'll help Bernadette and Jenn through this, but we'll do it after you've fulfilled the obligation we have to our families. Do you understand?"

"Yes."

"You're going to suck it up and do what needs to be done to get through the next few hours."

"I will."

"Good. Now look at me," Paula snapped. I looked at her and realized there were tears in her eyes as she tried to stay stern. "You walk down that aisle and focus on Christopher. Let everything else fall away when you see him. He's never going to forget what you look like as you walk toward him. Don't let him down. Don't let your brothers down. Put your fucking crown on and hold your head high."

I took a deep breath and nodded at my best friend, knowing how much it hurt her to be so harsh with me when she was just as torn up about today's unexpected turn of events as I was.

"Are you okay?" I asked, breaking my resolve for a second.

"He's been dead to me for years, Frankie. A little blood doesn't bother me at all."

"But it will later, won't it?"

"Get going and shut the fuck up. We've got a wedding to attend, and I refuse to have red, puffy eyes and mascara running down my face for pictures."

I lifted my chin again and gave her a haughty smile. "Get your shit straight and blink those tears away, Paola. I won't have you looking like a raccoon as a member of my wedding party."

I addressed our friends who were standing around in stunned silence, "When the reception is over and the photographer is gone, we're going to get together and have a good, old-fashioned meltdown. Okay, ladies?"

I knew Maylee understood exactly what I was doing when she closed her eyes and sighed. She took a few calming breaths and a serene expression came over her as she straightened her posture and rolled her neck around before she let her shoulders relax. She opened her eyes and smiled at me, and I knew I was looking at the Maylee who had lived through hell and come out a winner on the other side, not the mom who had been terrified for her daughter's life an hour ago.

"Bernadette, Jenn, can you two handle this?" I asked. "There won't be any hard feelings if . . ."

"I'm fine, Frankie," Jenn said with a serene expression on her face. She gave me a sweet smile and looked over at Bernadette. "How about you?"

"We all look fantastic. We're going to walk down the aisle to our men and blow everyone in that room away."

"Damn right," Blue encouraged. "You look good, sister-in-law. Stunning."

"Let's do this," Brea said with a nod. She put her hand out and grinned at me. "No one fucks with the crazy coven and gets away with it. Am I right?"

"Hell yeah," Matalie said as she put her hand on top

of Brea's. I put mine on hers and the rest of our friends followed suit.

"Let's get you married, Big City," Blue said with a teasing grin as she put her hand on top of ours. "New York's not gonna know what hit it."

"I never imagined I'd have a tribe of women like you around me, but I wouldn't trade a single one of you for all the gold in the world." I looked around at the women who had become my family, my sisters. "I love all of you more than you'll ever know. Now cue the music bitches! It's time to make our grand entrance."

There were cheers and excited hoots as Bernadette lined the women up in front of my nephew and young cousin. I took a deep breath and exhaled slowly as I heard the music start inside the ballroom. I watched as, one by one, the women who I'd come to love as sisters disappeared through the doors until it was finally Olivia and Freddy's turn to go.

As soon as I heard the music change, I took a few steps and then stopped in the middle of the doorway as everyone in the room stood and turned around to look at me. I didn't see any of them, though, only Christopher at the front of the room, staring at me in awe, as if I were the most beautiful woman he'd ever seen.

Today, I was going to walk down the aisle and get my fairytale prince.

20

PAULA

"Who is that girl dancing with my son?" I asked my brother, Rico, as he led me around the dance floor to the waltz playing over the speakers. "She's gorgeous."

"That's Siobhan O'Sheeran. She's Darragh's sister," Rico explained. "The twins' dates are also from the O'Sheeran family. Cara is here with Luca and Aisling is accompanying Matteo for the evening."

"Are they dating?"

"No, they just hit it off and became fast friends. The boys know not to mix business with their personal lives."

"They do, huh?" I asked dryly. "Their entire lives will . . . *already* . . . revolve around business."

"I know, Paola," Rico agreed. "They'll work it out. We're going to watch out for them. So will the Romanos."

"What did you do with our father?" I asked after I'd looked around to make sure we weren't close enough for anyone else to overhear.

"That's a work in progress, little sister," Rico hedged.

"He's not just going to disappear, is he?" Rico smiled and shook his head. "That wouldn't be . . . dramatic enough, would it?"

"I don't think so."

"Oh, I can't wait." I laughed for a second as I imagined what I would do in their situation and then decided to give my big brother a few suggestions. "You know women are more cunning and devious than men give them credit for, right?"

"Of course," Rico agreed.

"I have a few ideas that I think would make a dramatic statement for any others who might be inclined to prefer the old ways."

"Do tell," Rico said with a laugh as he spun us around. "I'm all ears."

"Well . . ." I paused dramatically and grinned. "My first idea is going to require some breaking and entering and quite a bit of stealth."

"I'm afraid that your penchant for drama and revenge is wasted in Texas," Rico said with a sigh.

"Oh no, big brother. I've had plenty of chances to use my gifts, and I'm sure I'll have plenty more."

"Then tell me, Paola, if you were in charge, what would you do?"

I giggled and then gave him a few ideas on how I'd let this situation play out. By the time I was finished, so was the song. However, it took a little while longer for his shock to go away. I knew he was going to take my suggestions to the other men of the Four Families.

I might not be part of this lifestyle anymore, but I hadn't forgotten all the things it taught me. That was for damn sure.

STAMP

"Are you doing okay, Birdie?" I asked before I spun us around and then continued dancing while I waited for my girl to answer.

After a few long seconds with a hint of a smile, she stared up at me and said, "I couldn't be any better."

"I mean about earlier, sweetheart. How are your . . ."

"I knew what you meant, and I'm serious. It was terrifying, but I don't have any regrets. I did what needed to be done to help my friends and make sure that Boo was safe. If I had to do it all again, I wouldn't hesitate."

"I was shaken to the core when Matalie showed up," I admitted. "All the guys were, but there wasn't anything we could do."

"We took care of the problem. I know that if Jenn and I hadn't been outside, things would have played out differently, but the girls seemed to have a plan."

"What do you mean?"

"The way they were moving and getting his attention, it reminded me of that nature documentary we watched about lion prides and how they hunt."

"I remember." I nodded as I thought back to that night and the show we'd watched about the big cats. "The women made you think of that?"

"Yeah. The man . . . your uncle . . . was holding Boo under his arm. He was standing inside the living room, and they were fanned out in front of him. He had a gun, but he couldn't really cover all of them at once. They were talking to him as they inched forward, keeping his attention bouncing from one to the other and off of Boo."

"If you and Jenn hadn't come in behind him, they would have surrounded him and pounced."

"They would have," Bernadette agreed. "They didn't even plan it. They just did it . . . naturally."

"None of them are the kind to cower. You're not either. That's why you get along so well with them."

"They were flanking him and keeping his attention diverted."

"Just like the lions."

"Exactly like the lions. And do you remember what happened when they got a hold of that buffalo?"

"They ripped him apart."

"They'd have done that. And I would have helped."

"Does that upset you?"

"Realizing what I would do if someone in my family

was threatened?"

"Yeah."

"When I was alone and threatened, all I could think to do was run. But when I'm with them, I know I don't have to do that."

"You'll never have to run again, Birdie. I'll make sure of it."

"And so will my girls," Birdie said with a grin.

"You're right." I couldn't help the chuckle when I thought of the comparison, and Birdie looked at me in confusion so I had to explain. "It's kind of like the mafia, if you think about it."

"What . . . our coven?"

"Yeah. Once you're in, you're in. They've got your back just like you've got theirs. They've proved themselves over and over. A few months ago, when Sis was kidnapped, Brea and Blue chased the fuckers who'd taken her instead of losing their shit or cowering in fear. When they caught them, it was all over. What happened today was the same sort of thing, but all of you were involved. Someone threatened the family, and rather than play the role of damsels in distress, you took care of business. The man that loves you is still freaking out at the thought of losing you, but the man I was raised to be is just chilling because he knows that's what needed to be done."

"And we did what needed to be done."

"You did, Birdie, and even though the thought of you,

or any of the women, in danger strikes terror deep in my soul, I know that you can take on the world together."

Birdie grinned smugly. "The coven is unstoppable."

"And if they ever need backup, they've got all of us. My boys adore you and so does Paula's son. So not only do you have a whole group of crazy women by your side, you've got a bunch of ex-cons and mobsters watching your back too."

"I'll never have to run again." Birdie sighed, and I felt her relax in my arms as she rested her head on my chest. I held her close as we moved around the dance floor and smiled when I heard her say, "It's a good feeling."

"Isn't it, though?"

BOSS

"Does your hand hurt, or are you giving someone hand signals?" I asked as I felt Jenn clench and unclench her fist at my back.

"I guess I sort of tweaked it when I landed earlier."

I couldn't help but to shake my head and growl when I imagined her midair, 90 stories above the ground. She sighed and said, "I shouldn't have said anything. We were having such a nice evening."

"I'm not mad," I assured her.

"Bullshit."

"Okay, I'm not as mad as I was earlier."

"You just growled."

"I love you, Jenn. The thought of losing you makes me crazy. When I imagined what you went through today, and I wasn't there to help . . . I'm not good at being useless."

"You aren't useless! You weren't even there!"

"Kitty had a good suggestion earlier and . . ."

"Was that before or after your dance party?" Jenn teased.

"I only dance with you."

Jenn smiled and then put her hand behind my neck and pulled me down for a kiss. "I'm okay. Boo's okay. My friends are okay. I need you to be okay too."

"I can't let you out of my sight. Someday, you and those girls are going to get up to something and give us all fucking heart attacks worrying about you."

"We worry about all of you too."

"We need a moat. Full of alligators with snipers on every corner. We'll keep our families inside so we know you're safe."

"That makes absolutely no sense."

"The more I think about it, the more it sounds like a reasonable idea."

"One of us would get eaten by a gator trying to escape, and knowing me, I'd probably fall off the wall like Humpty Dumpty. Then what would you do?"

"You make me crazy, woman."

"I love you, Boss. I'll try really hard not to worry you in the future."

"You say that, but then . . ."

"Circumstances outside my control tend to happen, and knowing our family, that's not going to change anytime soon. Maybe I should go ahead and find a cardiologist for you."

"You think you're funny, but I'm not fucking laughing."

"I'm laughing because if I don't, I will melt down right here. It's been a rough day, but we made a pact to keep our shit together until this is over. If you keep growling and reminding me of what happened today, I'm gonna lose it, and I don't want to do that."

"What do you need me to do?"

"I need you to hold me now and then again later when I get the chance to fall apart."

"I can do that. I'll do anything to make you happy."

"I'll make a deal with you that's guaranteed to make you happy."

"What's that?"

"I'll never jump from one terrace to another again, even if it's on the ground floor. I promise." I stared down at her trying to resist putting her over my shoulder and carrying her back to the room to spank her ass for scaring the shit out of me, and she pushed me even closer to doing it by laughing. "You just growled again, caveman."

"You know what?"

"What?"

"Fuck appearances. I'm done."

"Huh?"

I pushed Jenn away from me and spun her around twice to throw her off. By the time she was facing me again, I was bent over in front of her, poised to do what I'd been thinking about for the last few hours.

I stood up and started walking toward the exit with Jenn over my shoulder. When she started squirming, I slapped her on the ass and she squealed loudly.

"Put me down!"

"No," I said with another slap to her backside.

I wove through the other dancers and made my way around the table full of our friends without saying a word. I heard their laughter and cheers behind us and couldn't help but smile. Every one of my brothers was envious of my position right now and wished like hell they could do the same thing, but it wasn't my fault they didn't have the balls to take what they wanted.

Because that was exactly what I was doing. I was

going to take Jenn upstairs and keep her safe while I showed her exactly how much I loved her. And then, when she was relaxed and satisfied laying safely in bed beside me, I might be able to breathe again.

Until the next time she scared me to death. And knowing her and that group of women, I had no doubt that would happen again and again.

BUG

"How'd she do?"

Hammer looked up at Maylee and smiled. "She was fine all evening."

"Did she eat? Was she upset?"

"Oh, she wasn't upset at all. Just her normal funny self."

Maylee sighed with obvious relief as she sat next to Hammer and rested her hand on Boo's back. "Do you think she'll remember what happened today?"

"I'd bet today was more traumatic for you than it was for her. She probably doesn't remember a thing about this afternoon," Hammer reassured her. "We played together and then I got her and Jared to watch a movie with me and have a snack before bedtime."

"So she ate dinner and then a snack?"

"Are you afraid she's gonna go on a hunger strike or something?" Hammer asked.

"No, but when she's sick or upset, she won't eat."

"Well, she ate plenty tonight. I promise." Hammer watched Maylee study our daughter, relaxed in sleep, with her mouth open and a spot of drool on Hammer's t-shirt. "We had pizza for dinner, then popcorn, gummy worms, and some ice cream while we watched the movie."

"Oh," Maylee said with wide eyes. "That's . . . good."

"She loved it. So did Jared. There's some leftover pizza in the fridge, but we plowed through the rest."

"I'm sure. What did you watch?"

"*Friday.*"

"Today's Saturday."

"No, we watched *Friday.*"

"Today? Huh?"

"It's an old movie, babe," I explained with a laugh as I shook my head. Hammer's movie choices weren't really appropriate for toddlers, but hopefully, what Hammer said was true, and Boo wouldn't remember anything about this day.

"Oh. I guess I missed that one. Where's Jared?"

"He's asleep in the bedroom. I carried him in there so she wouldn't wake him up while we watched the second movie."

"What was next? *The Texas Chainsaw Massacre?*" I asked with a pointed look.

"God no. If I was going to start her on anything, it would be the *Friday the 13th* franchise. What kind of man do you take me for? Jeez," Hammer said with disgust. "We watched *Gremlins.*"

"The little furry animals?"

Hammer nodded in response to Maylee's question and then asked, "Can you get her off of me? I've been afraid to move because I didn't want to disturb her, but I've gotta piss so bad that my eyeballs are floating."

Maylee laughed softly and reached out to take Boo. "I'm going to put her in our bed. She can sleep with us tonight."

Hammer got up from the couch and leaned down to kiss Boo's forehead and then Maylee's before he murmured, "She's fine, Mama. She's just fine."

"I'm not," Maylee said as her eyes filled with tears. "I'm not okay at all. I'm going to go lay down with her. Thank you for watching her for us, Hammer."

"Anytime, babe."

We watched Maylee go into the master bedroom and shut the door behind her. I looked over at Hammer and said, "Thanks, man. I know we'd both rather have been with her but . . ."

"The kids were fine. I was glad to stay here and hang out."

"Kitty and Pandora are still at the reception with the girls, but they have a key to our room. They'll come get Jared when they're finished."

"Fuck . . . I've gotta piss. Go be with your old lady, and I'll see myself out."

"Thanks again, Hammer."

"Hey, we're family. That's what family does, watch out for each other, right?"

"Yeah."

"Go dry her tears and cuddle up with them. I'm good."

I nodded and slapped him on the shoulder as he walked past me to the hall bathroom and I made my way into our bedroom.

Maylee was still in her bridesmaid dress, laying beside Boo as tears streamed down her cheeks. I laid across from her and reached out to dry her face before I asked, "Why don't you go take a shower and wash your face, babe? I'll lay here with her."

"Watching that man hold Boo today was the most terrifying thing that's ever happened to me, and I've seen some shit in my life, Enzo."

"I'm sure you have."

"For years, I made sure to guard my heart and never let anyone get too close, then I met her and she changed my whole life."

"I know the feeling."

"And you did the same thing." I smiled at her, and she laughed softly. "Must be genetic."

"Must be," I agreed. "I can't imagine my life without the two of you in it."

"I know it started out . . . rough, but things have changed between us over time."

"They have."

"We're different now, and it's all because of Boo."

"Things are different in the best way. She was a surprise, and so were you."

"Me? I guess I didn't really come off as the maternal sort, huh?"

"You took care of your girls, and I see that now, whereas before, I didn't recognize it. But the way you are with Boo . . . and with me is a side of you I never imagined."

"How so?"

"When we got married, it was all about Boo, but things are different now. I wouldn't change a thing about my life."

"You never thought you'd be married with a kid, huh?"

"I never thought I'd be head over heels for my wife either, but that's what happened." Maylee's eyes widened as she stared at me in shock. I continued, "It made my blood run cold when I found out what happened with that man today and not just because Boo was in danger. You were imperiled, too, and the thought of losing you nearly paralyzes me with fear. I love you Maylee, and I can't imagine my life without you in it."

"I love you too."

"Now go wash off your war paint and get comfortable. I'll stay here with our girl, then we'll snuggle up together and get some rest."

"I don't think I can sleep."

"Then you can lay here in my arms, and we'll watch our little girl dream, okay?"

"Okay."

I leaned over Boo's sleeping form and gave my wife a kiss. "I really do love you, Maylee."

"And I love you."

21

FRANKIE

"Are you ready yet?" Christopher called out from the living area. "We were supposed to be there 10 minutes ago!"

"You knew exactly what you were getting into when you proposed to me, Christopher. Why are you yelling all of a sudden?"

"This is exactly what men are warned about all their lives. You put a ring on it and everything changes," he said as his eyes roamed from my head to my boots and back up again. "Although, I put the ring on the most beautiful woman in the world, so I'm okay with it."

"This is vacation Frankie," I reminded him. "Work Frankie likes to be early, but vacation Frankie doesn't really care. And just so you know, we'd have been on time if you hadn't joined me in the shower."

"The sounds you were making sure didn't sound like complaints," he boasted as he slowly walked toward me. I could tell by the look on his face that he was about to try and make us *much* later, so I held my hand out and shook my head. "Come on. Vacation Frankie doesn't give a shit, remember?"

"All of my personalities care right now because I'm a

little tender in some places that need a little rest, if you know what I mean."

Christopher's grin was cocky as he slowly nodded. "Hell yeah. Wore it clean out, didn't I?"

"You clearly know nothing about female anatomy," I grumbled as I turned to go back into the bedroom and put on my jewelry.

Christopher caught me around the waist and pulled me back into his body right before he nipped at my neck with his teeth. "I clearly do or you wouldn't have let me do all those things to you last night and then again this morning."

I couldn't suppress the shiver his gravelly voice so close to my ear caused, and I felt myself melting into his arms.

"Nope! Not gonna do it!" I said as I pushed away from him and rushed into the bedroom. "Keep your hands and lips away from me for at least four hours, mister."

"Four hours?" Christopher asked as he leaned against the door frame and watched me. "I can deal with four. Maybe."

I smiled at his reflection and teased, "If I can last that long, you can too."

"Why are you getting all fancied up if we're just going to breakfast?"

"We have one more adventure we can't miss," I explained. "I promised the girls we'd take the subway, and we haven't been able to do that yet."

"*That's* what we're doing today?"

"If the girls are up for it, then yes, that's what we're doing today. After yesterday, I'm sure the guys aren't going to let us out of their sight, so that means you're probably going with us."

"Yeah, I'm not sure when this feeling's going to go away."

"What feeling?"

"Mind-numbing terror is probably the best description for it. I'll probably feel better once we get back to Texas, but I can't guarantee it."

"The girls and I can take care of ourselves, sweetheart. You know that." I shrugged and tried to pretend I wasn't affected by yesterday's events when I said, "We were working our way around him to get the gun and then we'd have taken care of the problem ourselves."

"One or more of you would have gotten shot in the process," he said angrily. "That is not acceptable odds."

"It was more acceptable than Boo getting hurt," I reminded him honestly. Christopher sighed and looked down at the carpet, unable to come up with an argument for that statement. "I have to give the girls one last fun memory of Manhattan because I'm positive Preacher's not going to ever let your sister come back. You know how he is."

"If it was anyone else, I'd laugh at the thought of someone telling her what to do, but she'll do what Preacher asks. She might not do it quietly, but she'll do it."

"She doesn't know how to do anything quietly."

"Good point."

"Okay, I'm ready to go," I said as I picked up the purse I'd chosen for today. "Don't forget your coat. There's snow in the forecast."

"Another reason I'm glad we're going home in the morning," Christopher griped. "This weather is bullshit."

"I'll remind you of that when you're bitching about the heat next summer."

BREA

"That was fun in a very unsanitary and smelly way," I admitted as I waited with Blue and Jenn at the top of the stairs. We watched as the rest of our friends made it up and joined us, and then I asked, "Now what's the surprise you have on our schedule?"

"We're going to get some coffee at a cafe I love, and then we're going to walk through the park back to our hotel."

Blue sighed as she glared at Frankie. "It's fucking cold out here. What happened to those Town Cars you love so much?"

"Ages ago, Jenn mentioned that there's a statue in the park that she really wanted to . . ."

"The Alice in Wonderland statue!" Jenn shouted as

she bounced up and down. "You remembered!"

Frankie laughed and said, "Of course I did. Gunther's isn't far from the statue, so we can carry our drinks and see it on our way back."

"This is so awesome!"

I couldn't help but smile at Jenn's excitement and fell into step behind her and Boss as Marques reached for my hand.

"Are you warm enough, Pickle?"

"I am. This coat Frankie let me borrow is great. I'm glad I brought the gloves after all."

Marques put his arm over my shoulders and pulled me closer. "Do you feel a little better now? Still ready to go home?"

"I am. I miss the dogs and our house. I just want to relax for a few days once we get back. This week has been one thing right after another."

Chef agreed with a dry laugh. "Pretty sure yesterday soured me on this place for good."

"The whole town isn't bad, Marques. I've had a lot of fun," I admitted. "That's not to say I'll ever come back, but still . . ."

Chef's laughter interrupted me, and he said, "I'll bring you back whenever you're ready."

"I think I'm good."

"Are we still on for a romantic dinner tonight?"

"We are. I'm going to get dressed up one last time and let you take me out on the town."

"And then I'm gonna fuck you in the snow on our balcony."

I sputtered out a laugh and looked up at the man I love. "It's awfully cold. How about in front of the window overlooking the balcony?"

"We'll see, Pickle. We'll see."

JENN

"This has been on my bucket list for ages," I told Blue as we studied the statue in front of us. I lifted my camera and took another picture and then moved to the side for a better angle.

"We should have the guys take some shots of us with the statue," Blue suggested before she called out, "Brea, give your camera to one of the guys, and let's pose with the statue."

She handed her camera to Chef and joined us as we tried to figure out how to climb onto the statue.

"You know this story is just chock full of mental illness and drug abuse, right?" Preacher asked.

"Everyone knows that. It's not one of your life-ruining theories," I argued.

"The girl suffered from hallucinations, but did you know that some people wonder if it wasn't really a description of what happens when you have a migraine?" That was one I hadn't heard before, so I turned around and looked at Preacher and waited for him to continue. "Auditory and visual hallucinations can sometimes accompany severe migraines. Back in the day, opium was used to help cure headaches, which is most likely what that caterpillar was smoking in his hookah."

"Really?"

"Yep. I'm not throwing out the whole drug-induced hallucination thing, but it could be him describing what happened while he had really severe head pain. He was known to have intense headaches pretty often."

"How did I not know that?"

"Luckily, we've got Preacher here to give us all those unnecessary details," Captain teased.

"Fuck you," Preacher retorted as he flipped off our friend. "There are some other illnesses in it too. That rabbit had pretty bad anxiety, and the queen was a narcissist. The caterpillar was a drug addict, and the Mad Hatter was nuttier than a fruitcake."

"Can we start calling you Fruitcake?" Captain asked. "You're pretty goddamn nutty."

"How does this look?" I called out, interrupting the impending argument.

"Looks good, babe," Boss called out as he took out his phone. "Y'all smile!"

I smiled for the camera and waited as the guys all took pictures, and then we all made faces for a few shots before Blue started trying to figure out how to do a dirty pose with the rabbit and Brea climbed up to sit on Alice's head.

The guys were laughing just as hard as we were, and after a few minutes, we finally got back down, ready for the warmth of the hotel and our various plans for the evening.

I walked between Frankie and Blue and behind Brea, Paula, and Matalie as we talked about what we wanted to do in the city before we left in the morning.

"We're going on a date," Brea told us. "I'm going to get all gussied up one more time, and then I'll be ready to go home and get comfortable again."

"Hook and I are having dinner with Zach and my brothers," Paula told us. "Bernadette, are you guys going to hang out with the twins?"

"We are," Bernadette answered. "Stamp went to their penthouse this morning and put some sauce on to simmer."

"Christopher and I are going to have dinner with my brothers and their kids, but we should be done by nine if y'all want to hang out for a while," Frankie suggested. "We should get a car and go over the Brooklyn Bridge while it's dark so you can enjoy all the lights."

"Oh, that sounds good!" I agreed.

"They'll like that," Paula agreed. "If we're finished at

Zach's in time, I'll come too."

"We should invite Bug and Maylee," I suggested.

"I talked to her this morning at breakfast, and she said that they were going to stick to their suite with Boo until we go home," Bernadette told us.

"I'm going to sedate my girls to get them on the plane in the morning," Pandora complained. "They've had so much fun with all the other teenagers that . . ."

"The boys," Blue teased, and I heard Kitty growl from somewhere behind us.

"Yes, the boys, although they have made some really good friends in Ziggy and Relio's girls too. They're planning to stay in touch, and the girls have already asked if we can have them down in the summer."

"That would be fun. I'd love to have my nieces visit. My nephews, too, if they're willing." Frankie bumped into me and knocked me back causing Paula to slam into my back, and I heard her yell, "He's got my purse!"

"Oh shit!" Blue yelled right before she started chasing the man. "Let's get him!"

Without even thinking, I started running after Blue right along with the rest of our friends. We tried our hardest to keep up, but the man was nimble as he darted around other clusters of people in the park.

It didn't take long before he was too far away for us to do anything. Blue stopped running and leaned forward to rest her hands on her knees as she tried to catch her breath. I did the same thing as Blue gasped, "Fuck it. I'll buy you a new purse. That bastard was fast."

"Shit," Matalie wheezed beside me. "I'm out of shape."

"Fuck all this running," Pandora panted. "Never again. I'll put in for the new purse, Frankie."

"I've got plenty at home," Frankie said as she put her hands up behind her head and paced back and forth like runners do after a race. "There wasn't anything important in it, so it's all good."

"Shouldn't we call the cops?" Brea asked, pulling her phone out of her pocket.

"Did you see what he looked like?" Boss asked as he helped me stand. He was barely winded. I wanted to punch him since I still couldn't breathe, and I was dripping sweat under my coat.

"Blonde, about six feet tall . . ." I started.

"The man had dark hair, Jenn," Blue argued. "And he was way over six feet."

"He was white. I got that much," Matalie added. "I think he was wearing a beanie."

"Dammit! I really wanted to catch him!" Blue exclaimed as she looked in the direction the man had gone.

"He's a mile away by now," Brea grumbled. "That fucker was fast."

"What do you think he looked like?" I asked Boss.

"White, over six feet tall . . . that's all I got." I studied Boss's face for a few seconds, wondering why he wasn't more upset that we'd chased a criminal through the park, when he smiled at me. "You were hauling ass, babe. Good job."

"You're not mad at me?" I asked as I looked around at the other men who were all trying to catch their breath.

"We were right behind you," Boss said as he put his arm around my shoulders.

"I dropped my coffee," Blue complained. "That sucks."

"Now we *really* have to find him and kill him," Preacher teased. Blue pushed at his shoulder and he grinned. "What? I'm on your side!"

"Let's get back to the hotel where it's warm, and we can try and agree on a description for the cops," Matalie suggested. "I'm freezing my ass off, even with my beautiful red cape."

"You looked like Superwoman hauling ass through Central Park," Paula teased. "When you vaulted over that dog, I almost cheered."

"I'm limber like that," Matalie boasted.

"I just want to go home," Pandora said as she hooked her arm through mine.

"Yeah, I think we've served enough time in New York City. We need to be released back into the wilds of Tenillo where it's warm," Blue suggested as she hooked her arm into Pandora's. Paula got in on the chain, and Brea was right beside her as Matalie and Frankie did the same. "I'm ready to go home where it's nice and peaceful."

I heard the men behind us laughing, and I couldn't help but join them. Peaceful or not, I was surrounded by my best friends and the men we loved, and that was my favorite place to be.

EPILOGUE

FRANKIE

"I'll get my assistant to put your package in the mail tomorrow," my brother said with a grin before he looked back down at the pan of onions sautéing on the stove in front of him. "Is everyone settled in at home now?"

"We're all glad to be back in Texas where the weather is at least tolerable. Just give the purse to Stan. I'm afraid if the ladies see me carrying it, they'll figure out we planned the whole thing."

I heard something behind me and spun around to see Christopher leaning against the doorframe with a big smile on his face.

"You arranged for someone to mug you in Central Park?"

"Actually, my brother did." I winced and then smiled sheepishly. "It was supposed to be a secret."

Federico started laughing, and when I looked back at my phone screen, I realized he'd picked up the phone, the pan on the stove forgotten as he said, "It was Frankie's plan, but I made it happen. You should have seen my guy's face when I told him what I wanted him to do."

"One of my brother's men is an avid runner. He

competes in the New York City Marathon every year," I explained.

"He's going to run in Boston next year too," Federico explained. "When I told him I wanted him to mug my sister and slow his usual pace down a little so they could get a good chase in before he put on the gas to get away, he stared at me like I'd lost my mind."

"Good grief. You're just as crazy as the rest of them," Christopher said as he pulled me into his arms. "Thanks for humoring her, Rico."

"They wanted an adventure, so I gave it to them," I explained with a grin before I looked back at my brother. "I'd do anything for my girls, even get mugged."

"I've got to finish dinner, Frank. I'm sure you'll hear from Constance as soon as I give her your purse."

"I'll talk to you soon," I told my brother before I told him I loved him and ended the video call. I looked at Christopher and said, "You can't tell them it was a setup or it will take away from the magic of the experience."

"Only the coven would consider getting mugged a magical experience."

I grinned. "Your sister wanted to chase a mugger through Central Park so I made sure she got the opportunity."

"You're all nuts."

"But you love me."

"More than life itself, Big City. I always will."

THE END

COMING SOON

Sin (The Tempests, Book 7) - COMING DECEMBER 15th, 2022!

Sin Tempest has spent her adult life in the shadow of the tragedy that thrust her family into the spotlight in the worst possible way. After years spent in the protective circle of her siblings, she fell in love with the wrong man and was gradually sucked back into the same awful situation she'd endured as a child. As much as they tried, the Tempests couldn't manage to break Sin free.

After years away from her family, tragedy strikes and they're back by her side as they band together to escape the unwanted attention that has found them again. Old friends that are more like family come to the Tempests' rescue once more, and Sin and her family find refuge in a place that's almost too good to be true.

Now facing public scrutiny and trying to raise her little family on her own, Sin has to learn that the mistakes of her past don't have to decide her future if she'll just give love one more shot.

Blaze Westland ran from his small hometown to escape the expectations that were thrust on him after his father's death. When his beloved grandfather falls ill, Blake is called home. After making a deal with his grandfather in exchange for a life-saving surgery, Blaze settles into the role he was always meant to take.

Years ago, when he was still just a child, Blaze fell in love. Now, as an adult, he has the opportunity to make the dream he'd had years ago a reality, but he's got to convince the woman he loves to take a chance on him.

Join Cee Bowerman for the last book of the Tempests series, and get ready for the next chapters of the families you've come to love.

*****Please check the author's webpage and look for the blog post with the same title as this book. The author's note at the beginning of the book will also give you helpful information before you start reading. The details you find there might make a difference in how you enjoy this story.*****

About the Author

Cee Bowerman is proud, lifelong resident of Texas. She is married to her own long-haired, tattooed biker and is the proud mom to three mostly adult kids - a daughter and two sons. She believes in love, second chances, rescue dogs, and happily ever after.

Cee received her first romance novel along with a bag of other books from her granny when she was recovering from surgery at 15. She has been hooked on reading romances ever since. For years, she had a dream of writing her own series of stories, but motherhood and all the other grown up responsibilities kept getting in the way. Luckily, with the support of her family and the encouragement of her son, she purchased a computer and let her dreams become a reality.

Made in the USA
Middletown, DE
05 February 2025

70911667R00166